J.B. REDEL

Wyrds of Wonder

A Collection of Short Stories

Dedicated to my husband, Arthur, who has always been my biggest supporter; even when forced to suffer through countless hours of my storytelling.

Contents

Acknowledgement ii

CONTENT WARNING 1

Purgatory's Blade 2

The Gloomweaver's Gift 25

Shatter 39

Ashes of Innocence 48

Distant Hearts 58

Subconscious Convictions 66

Verdant Touch 76

Man-Made Morals 100

Fireheart 110

The Covenant of Redemption 125

Watchers 136

Enkindled 148

Ever Northward 157

The Midnight Sonata 168

For You 176

Hope's Haven 187

The Demon Within 197

Liberty's Freedom 207

Chiaroscuro of the Heart 220

Echoes of Madness 232

About the Author 245

Acknowledgement

Sometimes, the greatest accomplishments arise from the darkest circumstances. My love for writing emerged as I attempted to find a way to cope with night terrors. The method that stuck was journaling. Each morning, I would open my little blue notebook and jot down my dreams from the previous night. At first, I only wrote about the bad ones. But as I continued to journal, it became less of a chore and instead a hobby I looked forward to, even jotting down notes about the good and silly dreams.

I began using dreams as a writing prompt to create adventures.

Over the years, I struggled to satisfy my desire to write as I couldn't think of what to write about. My dream has always been to publish my own stories, but I wasn't ready to tackle a full-blown novel. That was when ReedsyPrompts came to my rescue!

Reedsy is a fantastic platform for new and developing authors. In addition to providing weekly prompts (which I have based on quite a few of my short stories), they provide courses, blogs, and writing software.

As I continue to learn more about writing, I hope to publish at least one more anthology while I work on my first fantasy novel.

CONTENT WARNING

Some of the stories in this anthology contain references to the following:

- Graphic or explicit violence
- Self-harm, suicide, or suicidal thoughts
- Mentions of sexual violence
- Abuse
- Gun violence
- Graphic descriptions of blood and other bodily fluids
- Death of/harm to a child
- Drug/alcohol abuse/addiction

Reader discretion is advised.

Purgatory's Blade

The night was silent save for horses' hooves pounding the packed dirt of the narrow trail as they raced down the path. Every muscle in Caine's body tensed as he leaned over the horse's neck, giving his mount every bit of lead he could without dropping the reigns altogether. His haggard breathing distorted his sight as he looked over to his brother, Ryler, riding alongside him.

Older by four years, his brother's features were hard, rarely showing any expression other than deep anger and fierce determination. A man of few words, verging on mute, Ryler believed his actions conveyed more meaning than words ever could. Sometimes, the two men would travel for weeks before the older man would utter a word.

Caine knew all too well who was responsible for the mask of near-constant anger that tainted his brother's features. Before Caine had even seen his sixth winter, he and his brother were forcefully taken from the warmth of their homes and thrown into intensive and torturous training by a shrouded and wholly unknown cult known as the Black Hand.

The cult had existed since before The Dark Age, a terrible time in history six hundred years past where disease both known and unknown to man sprung forth from seemingly nowhere and loosed itself upon all forms of life. Death washed over cities like a cold wave of desolation.

Unbeknownst to most of the world, the Black Hand were solely responsible for the beginning and end of The Dark Age. The cause of this sudden death and illness across the land was due to a large congregation of cultist members practicing arts, of which implications they were not wholly aware. While still a young organization, the Black Hand made up for their inexperience concerning the practice of dark arts with fierce and unwavering determination.

Blinded by such devotion, a deep wound was torn into the thin fabric separating the living world and a realm belonging to those who had already parted from the living. The rift between realms released twisted and tormented souls upon the world, free to wreak havoc unchallenged.

Belatedly understanding that the folly of tampering with realms better left undiscovered, the Black Hand turned their blind determination away from bringing forth dark entities to rectifying the disaster they brought forth. Having long since tossed aside their humanity in the pursuit of demonology and the arts of darker origin, the cultists were able to see that which untainted humanity could not. As such, whereas humankind struggled futilely against an invisible foe, Black Hand fought against demons and creatures whose tormented bodies took on forms too awful to describe.

Over nearly a century, the Black Hand fought from the shadows. In the beginning of what became known in cultist history as the Dark War, thousands of devoted members were sacrificed while practice of exorcism was perfected. With the constant need for new bodies to replace those that were lost, children were snatched from homes and brainwashed into blind faith to the cult.

Although children were not nearly as able-bodied as grown men and women, their minds were more susceptible to instill with the teachings of the Black Hand. Those who survived the indoctrination into the cult were either placed among scholars devoted to understanding of the realm whose border still needed mending or elevated to a higher form of training: demon hunting and exorcism. The survivability of such training was lower than that of an actual exorcism. Though it lacked timeliness and yielded few hunters over several years, the rigorous training proved effective. The few demon hunters who survived the training were considered the devout among the cult, if not the deadliest.

As the ranks of the Black Hand grew, so did the knowledge of this newfound land of the afterlife, aptly called The Depths for its seemingly boundless realm. Finding a way to close the tear between worlds cost the cult thousands of lives and required experimentation with arts darker than that which had caused the initial fissure. By the time the breach slowly began to repair, the world had been irrevocably changed.

Entire nations stood divided and at arms, each blaming another for the downfall of the world and would have waged war had they had the able bodies to do so. Walls were erected around cities to keep those tainted with disease and plague from entering. Refugees were deemed contaminated and were often turned away or killed at the gate of whichever town or city they begged to be allowed into.

What were once grand cities became ruins picked clean by the few scavengers who were fortunate enough to avoid succumbing to sudden illness.

During the repair of the fissure between worlds, a less

corrupt realm was discovered. This discovery served as a passable link between the physical world and The Depths. This realm became known as Purgatory. Here, souls were brought to be judged upon the actions of their mortal life. If deemed unworthy by some unknown authority, the sinful souls were forced into eternal pain and suffering in The Depths. Only speculations could be determined on what happened to those deemed worthy to avoid everlasting torment.

Despite best efforts to mend the fissure between realms, too long had the gate from The Depths stood open and allowed demons to flood forth. Though a majority of the tormentors had been exorcised and removed from the world of the living, evidence of their existence continued upon the world, resulting in the need for more bodies to serve the Black Hand and their newfound purpose of exorcism and study of The Depths. For this reason were Caine and Ryler indoctrinated into the cult.

Fifteen long and painful years filled with rigorous training passed before the brothers earned the title of demon hunters.

Though the trials they endured were the same, their bodies and personalities developed into complete opposites. In this regard, they made up for each other's shortcomings. Ryler's body grew to tower above most. He easily stacked on muscle, lending him the strength to crush men with his bare hands should he find himself without a weapon. Rather than observe his quarry from a distance, he rushed headfirst into battle, crushing his foes with brute force.

On the other hand, Caine struggled to gain height and muscle, his head barely reaching to his brother's broad shoulders. Rather than fight with brawn, of which he had none, he used his small stature to attack unseen from the shadows. With a more diminutive stature than average men, he took advantage of his lack of presence, blending in with his surroundings to watch his prey and find his advantage without their knowing.

Rather than wielding large and fearsome weapons as Ryler did, Caine lined every hand-stitched pocket within the confines of his robes with blades of various shapes and sizes.

Even the grooming standards between the two brothers were in complete contrast. Where Ryler kept the hair atop his head trimmed short as to avoid his foe the advantage of grabbing a handful in hand-to-hand combat, Caine cared little for grooming habits and let his black curly hair grow to a considerable length. He occasionally took a blade to it to keep Ryler's disappointed expression at bay. At times, he would purposely cut it unevenly just so that it might irritate his brother. Comparing their numerous differences, few believed they were indeed kin.

Not only were they completely different from one another, but there was one large factor that kept them apart from other demon hunters. They were never brainwashed into complete devotion. Perhaps it was due to the fact that they had each other, whereas few other children who advanced to demon hunter training had surviving siblings. Though they lacked unwavering devotion to the Black Hand, in fact they despised the cult and all that it had done to them, they carried out their assignments with fervor. They had no choice; no one leaves the Black Hand. At least not while alive.

Caine never feared death, as it meant his freedom from the life he never wanted. And yet… he couldn't leave Ryler to the machinations of the cult without him. Ryler wasn't an idiot, which most assumed due to his lack of speech, but he lacked Caine's calculating mind.

Gathering his courage, Caine glanced behind them and down the dark trail as their horses sped through the night. The path lay bare, allowing a faint hope to spark in his chest. They were rapidly approaching the boundary that separated the world of the living from Purgatory. Recalling the events that led them to the position they now were in, he cursed the Black Hand for giving them this assignment.

The current King, Rowan Wulfric, was not known for his compassion and ruled his Kingdom with cruelty and military force. His only daughter, Princess Abigail, having recently passed her sixteenth year, met her untimely demise at the hands of a group of men seeking to use the child as leverage. They sent word to the King that she would be unharmed and returned should he reward them with an ample amount. Enraged, the King feigned compliance, sending his men to retrieve his daughter under the guise of a hand-off. Strict orders were given that, along with the return of Abigail, the assailants were to be detained for punishment. During the skirmish, not only did the men take their own lives, but Abagail's as well.

King Wulfric had all but gone insane with grief at the loss of his only daughter. Unable to accept her passing, the brothers were brought forth and hired to pass into Purgatory. How the King knew of Purgatory and The Depths, he didn't know. Their mission had been to scour the bridged land between the living and The Depths in search of the girl's soul. If found, they were to bring her back across. Never had such an act been attempted nor even considered.

Ryler and Caine had crossed the border over a week ago, unsure of what they would find but confident nonetheless. Other than a lingering sense of wrongness, there was no apparent difference between the world of the living and Purgatory after passing the veil. Two days of travel brought the brothers to their first encounter. Nestled in a small clearing at the foot of an extensive mountain range, they came across a small village. The cottages and buildings that made up the community showed centuries of neglect, most structures falling apart where they stood. The most unsettling aspect of the village was the people. Men, women, and children of all ages occupied the small cottages and overgrown roads in between. As the brothers approached the village, the residents did not move, seemingly unaware of the outsider's approach. They stood silently, facing the same direction and sharing the same lifeless look.

Ryler reached behind his back and loosened his giant battle axe from its restraint, glancing cautiously around at the village's occupants while Caine dismounted and made his way to the nearest woman. She looked to be in her mid-thirties. Her simple burlap dress and the beads braided into her hair looked similar to the ancient civilizations he was taught about as a child. Glancing around the village, he noted that all the townsfolk were dressed from different eras. The outfits ranged from as old as the woman before him to as modern and elegant as the noblemen who walked the grand halls of King's Court today.

Despite his attempts to get her attention, the woman would not acknowledge his presence. Frustrated, he moved on to the next closest person. The older man wore a more modern garb similar to a tradesman's. He had just as much luck trying to get a response from him as he did with the ancient woman. Next was a young girl who looked to have seen no more than six winters. The simple white nightgown she wore was torn

8

nearly to shreds, a dark purple ring of bruises wrapped around her neck. He tried not to think what might have caused her untimely death as he knelt beside the girl so that he was at her eye level.

"Excuse me, little one." He said, keeping his voice soft. She continued to stare ahead with the same lifeless gaze as the others. He shifted uncomfortably, swallowing back against the dread rising in his chest. He was uncomfortable around children to begin with, and he couldn't decide if knowing the girl was already dead and wouldn't run crying to her parents made him feel better or worse.

"Have you seen another young girl around here? She is about as tall as my shoulders, with long auburn hair. She goes by the name of Abigail Wulfric?"

Behind the young girl, a few yards away, movement caught Caine's attention. A middle-aged man dressed in a simple farmer's garb had turned to look directly at him. Something about his gaze made Caine uneasy. As he glanced around the crumbling village, he noticed more people were looking in his direction. He turned back to the young girl before him. She, too, was looking directly at him. It was then that he noticed her eyes, or lack thereof. The sockets where her eyes were only moments before were now empty chasms of darkness.

The hair on his neck instantly stood on end as he quickly distanced himself from the girl. He had instinctively pulled free one of the larger knives hidden under his coat. Retreating another step, Caine crouched down, ready for an attack. No attack came. Experimentally, he sidestepped a few paces to the left. Faces of empty sockets followed his movement. He looked back to Ryler but only received the same hard features his brother always wore when waiting for Caine's next move.

9

A piercing scream filled the still air. The horses startled, and Caine barely managed to grab the reigns of his mount before the steed bolted. He tried to determine where the scream came from, but the sudden silence was so deafening that he questioned whether or not he had heard it in the first place.

The scream came again, this time closer and with an edge of agony. Sheathing his knife, Caine hopped onto his horse to gain better control. The giant horse stomped fearfully underneath him. Focused on scanning the nearby tree line, he nearly yelped when his brother's hand firmly gripped his shoulder, turning Caine back towards the village.

The people were gone. All that still stood were the crumbling cottages and deteriorating roads.

Sharing a glance, the brothers urged their horses back toward the trail they had been on before discovering the village. The horses were more than happy to comply, and the thickness of the forest quickly swallowed the ancient ruins as they raced away.

Although they left the village behind, the screaming persisted. The wails of agony never seemed any closer, but neither did it fade as they tried to put distance between themselves and the village. The shrill torment was a constant unwanted companion. Neither slept the following days, their nerves on end.

On the sixth day, Caine began hallucinating. Faces peeked out from between trees, just beyond his field of vision. No matter how quickly he turned to look, the faces were gone by the time his gaze settled on their location. Occasionally, the wind would pick up, carrying the whispers of voices. They called out to the brothers, making sweet promises and idle threats. Even stuffing moss in their ears to block out the noise proved futile.

Their sanity slipped more with each passing day, and at times, it seemed nothing could make their situation any worse. There is only so much that one's mind can take.

All at once, the screaming stopped. Rather than relax in the sudden silence, Ryler and Caine tensed and drew their weapons. They couldn't quite explain it, but the air felt heavier, setting their frayed nerves on alert. Scanning the darkness between the trees, Caine noticed his brother's gaze locked on something just past the tree line beyond their campsite.

At first, they couldn't tell what it was. Perhaps just a shadow or their mind playing another trick. But the shape seemed darker than the shadows surrounding them. The object paused for a moment before moving closer and emerging from the shelter of the trees. Three more emerged behind it.

The brothers stared at the approaching figures, unsure whether to stay and fight or run for their lives. It was not like them to hesitate under normal circumstances, but nothing about the situation they were in was normal. As the shapes slipped into the far reaches of the fire's light, they were finally able to assess this new threat. The figures hovered just above the ground. Shreds from their long, thin, torn cloaks ended with rusted shackles that dragged heavily on the ground. The sound of the metal links clinking together sent piercing chills down Caine's spine. They were tall and thin, with hoods pulled over their elongated faces. Only their hands were visible, protruding from the dark robes.

Long, thin fingers reached out toward the brothers, each multi-jointed digit ending in a dagger-like point. Tortured faces peered out from the darkness of their hoods, patches of rotting skin still clinging to bone. They moved slowly towards the men, a total of four of them. Caine knew they should run, but he felt frozen to the spot, his limbs ignoring any movement commands. He was still unsure if he was imagining these creatures or if they were real this time. The closer they drifted, the thicker the air became and the harder it was to breathe. His chest burned as his lungs begged for fresh air.

These creatures were not unknown to the Black Hand, though they were little more than a myth. The world of the living called them Reapers, tasked with carrying the souls of the departed through Purgatory. The air surrounding the demons carried disease, leaving a path of decay wherever they passed. They had never been seen in the land of the living before, as they were forbidden to pass through the border. It was rumored that a single touch from a Reaper, assuming their victim was still alive should the creature be close enough to touch, could split and fester skin upon contact.

The piercing scream erupted in the clearing. The wail so close that their ears were left ringing. Snapping out of his trance, Caine gasped for air. He hadn't realized that he had stopped breathing. He wiped his nose with the back of his hand as blood slowly streamed down his lips and dripped from his chin.

Ryler was still trapped in the breathless spell, blood slowly making its way from his nose. Caine grabbed the larger man's arm and dragged him to where their horses were tethered. Once he had managed to tear his gaze away, Ryler gasped for air as he mounted. Leaving their supplies behind, they kicked their horses into action and sped away from the hovering figures.

The night was silent save for horses' hooves pounding the packed dirt of the narrow trail as they raced down the path.

Every muscle in Caine's body tensed as he leaned over his horse's neck, giving his mount every bit of lead he could without dropping the reigns altogether. His haggard breathing distorted his sight as he looked over to his brother, Ryler, riding alongside him.

They headed directly for the border back towards the world of the living. Though they had spent just over a week in Purgatory, they had stayed relatively parallel to the border in case a quick escape became necessary. Caine was grateful then for the forethought.

As they bolted down the trail, he noticed bodies hanging from the trees. They appeared for only a second before disappearing. He focused on the ground ahead of his horse, staring directly between its ears at the trail before them. Only another mile or two, and they would be safe. He glanced at Ryler to ensure he hadn't fallen behind. Only the empty trail spread out behind Caine with no sign of his brother.

The horses' hooves dug into the ground as he pulled his mount to a quick halt, staring down the trail they had just come from. There was only one set of tracks from his horse in the dirt. Trying desperately to slow his breathing, Caine strained to listen. All he could hear was the labored breathing of his horse and the pounding of his own heart. Even the screams had ceased.

Caine took a deep breath, preparing to shout. He didn't have time to consider the implications of drawing attention to himself before he was cut short by the blood-curdling scream. This time, it was different. This time, it was deeper and familiar. This time, it was Ryler. The blood in his veins ran cold. He stared down the trail, trying to figure out how to proceed. He should go back for help. They were ill-prepared for this assignment, but they hadn't been sure what to expect in the first place.

Ryler screamed again, sounding further away. There wasn't enough time for Caine to fetch reinforcements.

Illumination from behind caught Caine's attention. Accustomed to the darkness, he had to shield his eyes as he searched for the source. Standing on the trail between Caine and the distant border was Abigail. She was dressed in a simple white gown, most likely the one she was buried in. An unnatural glow radiated from her, and her long brown hair swarmed slowly around her head as if underwater. Caine stared in shock at the apparition before him.

"A life for a life."

Her disembodied words filling his head made him cringe. It took another moment to process her meaning. To take her soul back to the world of the living, he had to sacrifice the soul of his brother. He heard Ryler scream again, further this time. He wheeled his mount around without a second thought and dug his heels into its sides. To hell with the King! Nothing was worth the life of his brother except his own.

Further down the trail, Caine found where his brother's tracks had stopped. It was as if he had vanished or was swept right off the ground. He spent only a moment searching for signs of Ryler's horse before heading toward his screams. He stayed on the trail as long as he could before being forced to dive headlong into the trees. The screams were beginning to sound closer and more frequent. Although each scream made Caine's blood freeze, at least that meant he was still alive.

Caine was suddenly pitched forward as his horses' legs tangled in the thick underbrush. The fabric on his sleeves tore at his futile attempt to cover his face as he fell into a thicket of dry, dead thorn bushes. They scraped and pulled at his skin as if trying to hold Caine down until he managed to untangle himself. He turned to retrieve his horse, only to find that his mount was being dragged underneath by the mass of vines and weeds that had tangled the horse's feet. Pulling one of his knives from his belt, he dove in after his horse.

Slashing and cutting through thick vines that moved like snakes, he almost had the beast free. He was jumping for the last thick vine, trying to avoid being trampled in the process, when a root the size of a grown man's thigh tore through the ground and raised itself above him. Before he could dodge, it swept around and slammed into his chest, sending Caine flying backward and landing hard against the trunk of another tree. The world went black. When he managed to open his eyes again, he couldn't make sense of the scene that played out before him.

Vines and roots popped from the ground surrounding his horse, almost completely submerged in withering vegetation. Once free of the ground, the roots wrapped themselves around what was still exposed of the animal and dragged it underground. Caine was thankful that the ringing in his ears drowned out the horse's squeals. He willed his body to move, to at least end the horse's suffering. A numb and tingling sensation had taken over his limbs, and he was helpless but to watch. The struggle was over within a minute. It was another minute before the feeling began returning to his limbs.

As the ringing in his ears dissipated, he realized he no longer heard Ryler's screams. Adrenaline brought Caine to his feet and he began running in what he hoped was the direction he had been heading before he fell. He did not have the slightest clue where he was running to, but he couldn't afford to sit and wait. Leaping away from reaching roots and dodging writhing vegetation, he had almost missed the tiny clearing. Stepping away from the tree line, he spied a singular, crumbling structure in the center. The building looked to have been abandoned, the remains consisting of stacked limestone and bricks. Behind the house was a small cellar door barely visible beneath the creeping vine slowly claiming the structure.

The closer he came to the cellar door, the harder it was to breathe as the air seemed to thicken. Dread rose from the depth of Caine's chest, and he was struck with a sudden coughing fit. Kicking the creeping vine aside, he pulled open the ancient wooden door, rusted hinges squealing in protest. He could see a few steps from the light of the moon high above the clearing, but beyond was pitch black. Taking a deep breath that could very well be his last, Caine stepped into the passage and was immediately engulfed in complete darkness.

With one hand on the wall to his left, he felt his way along the tunnel as it continued to lead down. He had no idea how long he walked before a light cut through the darkness. The orange hue was warm and inviting. At last, the tunnel evened out as he approached the light, which turned out to be a lone torch set in a sconce on the wall. Peering further down the tunnel, he saw only darkness. Not bothering to consider how or why the lit torch came to be there, he removed it from the sconce and continued, this time at least relieved to have some light guide his way.

Caine was confronted with the stench of rot so potent that he had to stop as he succumbed to another fit of coughing. He trekked on, covering his mouth and nose with the collar of his shirt. Another light broke through the dark. Rather than warm and inviting, an eerie blue glow that barely seemed to penetrate the surrounding darkness ebbed out from around a bend. He slowed his breathing as much as possible and stepped towards the light.

Past the bend, the tunnel opened into a large chamber. The source of the eerie blue light came from a well in the center of the room, which spouted a small fountain of fire. The flames were unnatural blue and purple rather than red and orange, and no heat came from the source. Lining the chamber walls were all manner of crude devices of stone and wood. Caine recognized a few from the Black Hand repentance room, where young cultists were sent to be punished and reflect on their transgressions.

The walls were made of solid stone, the surface marred by cracks and leaking moisture. Moss and fungus lined the walls and floors, claiming a few tables and shelves too close to the overgrown surface. Nothing grew on or near the well of cold fire. In several spots along the ceiling, cages hardly large enough for a grown man hung from rusted chains that squeaked as they swayed gently, seemingly of their own accord. As he glanced around the room, he thought he saw figures in the cages. When he looked again, he saw only rusted bars.

On the far side of the room, he finally found his brother. Ryler was tethered to a stretcher table, his wrists and ankles bound by roots and thorny vines. Caine dropped the torch and ran to him.

As Caine pulled at his brother's restraints, the thorns cutting deep into his fingers and hands, he noticed Ryler panting furiously. He, too, was having a difficult time drawing a breath. He searched for one of his knives but found none in their sheaths. He must have dropped them while trying to rescue his horse from the thickets. Cursing himself, he went back to frantically clawing at the vines. The vegetation only wiggled and tightened the more he pulled.

Caine froze. In his frenzy to release his brother, he hadn't noticed that Ryler was soaked in blood. His blouse and overcoat were missing. His pants were nearly torn to shreds. Blood slowly dripped from hundreds of long, thin cuts across his exposed skin, the blood pooling at the base of the table. The amount of blood on the floor alarmed Caine. Unless he staunched the bleeding somehow, it wouldn't be long before his brother lost consciousness. He retrieved the torch from where he had dropped it at the entrance to the chamber, hoping to burn the vines. He returned to his brother's side and noticed Ryler had stopped panting. He wasn't breathing at all.

A quiet, terrified squeak escaped his brothers' lips as he stared into the blue flames in the center of the room. His eyes were wide with horror, pupils fully dilated. Caine couldn't remember the last time he had seen such raw terror from his brother, not even when they were children being forced through the trials with the Black Hand.

Hissing came from behind Caine. The sound made what few hairs were not already standing on end move to do so. Whirling, he found the source of his brother's terror. The Reapers from earlier were emerging from the flames, their cloaks catching fire and burning around them. One of the Reapers took notice of the lit torch Caine held. Like a candle wick being blown out, the flame disappeared.

Caine tossed the unlit torch, more out of anger than anything else. It passed through the figures, whose bodies shifted like smoke at the disturbance. Caine grit his teeth and moved behind the table confining Ryler, trying to form a plan. They had to get out of there, and he wasn't leaving without his brother. Once free of the flaming well, the four figures moved no closer. They instead remained in still, watching him.

Cain's lungs burned and begged for air. He had almost entirely stopped breathing, not for lack of trying. Blood ran freely from his nose, and he could feel himself breaking out in a fever. The edges of his vision darkened as objects around the room lost their defined shapes. He backed up, trying to get as far away from these creatures as possible without leaving his brother behind.

A sharp point dug into his lower back as he found himself against the chamber wall. There had been a weapons rack he had not noticed before. The rack was pinned against the wall, and from it hung crude knives and blades. The largest was no longer than his forearm, the shortest as small as his finger. The blades were coated in a thick layer of rust and what Caine assumed was dried blood, their dull edges covered in nicks and dents.

"A life for a life."

Abigail appeared beside Caine, her skin illuminated in the same unnatural light from before, her hair swimming around her face. Her face lost its innocent, child-like features as his vision continued to lose focus. The tight skin around her face began to sag, her eyes sunk back into their sockets, and her hair thinned and fell away from her head, thought the strands continued to float around her. He stared, transfixed by what he was seeing. Is this what awaited them in the afterlife? If that was the case, he wanted more than ever to live.

Reaching behind his head, he grabbed the cloth-covered hilt of the largest knife he could reach. He doubted it would be much use as the blade's edge was dull and cracked. With one heavy swing, he cut through the restraints, holding one of Ryler's wrists. Not allowing himself to revel in his little victory, he made short work of cutting the rest of the vines. Ryler noticed Caine for the first time as he fell away from the table.

The hissing from the Reapers raised in pitch as they lurched toward the brothers. Supporting Ryler with his free shoulder, he waved the dull blade at the demons as he backed away. To his surprise, they stopped and recoiled, hissing louder, spittle flying from inside their hoods. Their reaction was not what he had expected, but he took advantage of their retreat.

With Ryler's arm around his shoulders and Caine supporting most of his weight, he moved quickly through the tunnel. The further they moved away from the chamber, the easier it became to breathe. He expected the Reapers to overcome them, considering how slowly they were moving, but they made it to the tunnels entrance with no confrontation. Caine slid the knife into one of the sheaths strapped to his thigh. It slid smoothly into the casing like it was made for the blade.

Finally, they emerged from the trap door behind the small cottage in the clearing. Ryler slipped from his grasp as Caine fell to his knees, exhausted. He felt like acid flowed through his veins and his heart would burst through his chest at any moment. They stayed there until their breathing had settled and Caine felt strength return to his legs. His vision was finally returning to normal, but there was still no sign of the Reapers.

He forced himself to stand and drape Ryler's arm around him. The bleeding from his wounds had slowed, but he had lost a dangerous amount of blood. He glanced around the clearing they stood in, trying to get his bearings. He had been in a panicked frenzy when he happened across the cottage and couldn't remember which direction he had come from.

A shrill cry sounded, seeming to come from every direction at once. With no more time to decide, Caine started them off in a random direction into the thick woods, hoping they were headed toward the border. He still didn't know how or why the creatures had not caught up to them, but he counted it as a blessing and continued picking their way through the thicket between the giant trees. Silently, Caine thanked every god he knew that the vegetation seemed satisfied with its earlier meal of horse flesh and did not come alive under their feet. Several times, he had to stop to catch his breath and make sure that Ryler was still alive, as his condition was worsening. His skin had lost all color, his breathing was shallow, and his skin felt cool to the touch. Caine feared that he would lose his brother before he had a chance to get him to safety.

Thankfully, Caine had picked the right direction, and they soon came across the road. At an agonizingly slow pace, they made their way to the border.

By the following day, they had reached the rift between worlds. Green mist settled over the ground, forming a barrier across the road and disappearing into the dense forest on either side. The swirling mists distorted his view of the other side, only the silhouettes of trees barely visible.

Abigail stood between the brothers and the border.

Her condition had not improved since he last saw her in the torture chamber. Her skin sagged from her bones like melted wax. Her eyes were so sunken into her skull that the sockets were empty. She stood hunched over as though stricken with old age. Her long, brown hair was gone, revealing a dimpled, bald head. Her gown hung limply from her atrophied body.

Ryler let out an agonized scream and fell to the ground, thrashing. Caine dropped down beside him, moving him to rest in his lap while he looked for any new injuries. Though Ryler thrashed in torment, Caine could see no obvious source of the pain.

"A life for a life."

Anger flared deep within Caine. If not for Ryler in his lap, he would have stood and charged the apparition.

Grabbing a nearby rock the size of his fist, he hurled it at the girl. It passed harmlessly through her and landed heavily on the other side of the border. The sound of the rock striking the ground came back muffled through the thick mist.

Ryler screamed louder then, his thrashing fiercer. The skin around his face started to sag, looking sickly and ashen. His eyes sunk back into their sockets, and his arms and chest muscles atrophied. The apparition laughed as the life disappeared from Ryler.

Abagail's young and healthy features returned as his brother's body wilted before his eyes. Her skin tightened over her face, her simple white gown filled out as muscle returned to her bones, and hair sprouted from her bald head. Clear brown eyes shined with delight.

All at once, Ryler stopped thrashing. He stopped screaming. He stopped breathing. Unbidden tears streamed down Caine's face as the only person in this world who knew or loved him died in his arms. Abigail continued to laugh, twirling in her gown and happily skipping around them.

Finally pulling his tortured gaze away from his brother's body, Caine looked up to find the four Reapers hovering before the border, watching as Abigail danced around the road, singing a child's folk song.

He had not seen them appear, though he didn't much care at the moment. Ryler was all he had in the world. Ever since they were taken from their family and thrown into hiding to be trained by the Black Hand, all they had was each other. Ryler had always been the stronger one, always by his side. Now, he had let his brother die. Now, he had nothing to lose.

Rage overwhelmed his loss and despair. Tears continued to stream down his cheeks, but his face held no emotion. As Abigail skipped by, giggling to the cloaked figures about how pretty she looked, Caine grabbed the cloth hilt of the knife he had taken from the chamber still tucked in his sheath. He lunged at her when she was only a foot away. The knife slid smoothly into her stomach, sinking to the hilt.

Abigail stared at Caine in confusion, which quickly morphed into hatred. As she reached for the knife, Caine pushed away from her, leaving the blade embedded in her stomach. The girl wildly flung her arms in an attempt to grab him, all the while howling at the top of her lungs. Caine recognized the agonizing scream. It was the same as the those that had plagued them. She continued to shriek and fell to the ground, convulsing. Her skin burned, blistered, and then turned to ash. The screams continued as the muscle in her body disappeared, her hair falling away from her bald head. Her voice was finally cut short by a wet gurgle.

Failing to feel any emotion, Caine watched as the body of the young girl deteriorated.

"Balance."

Caine was startled and turned toward the cloaked figures. He had forgotten they stood witness to all that had transpired. "What?"

They hissed again, forming nearly unintelligible words.

"A life for a life."

Behind him, Ryler gasped for breath. Spinning back, Caine

dropped to his knees beside his brother. His skin was still pale from lack of blood, but his face had regained some of its lost luster, and he gasped heavily for breath. Although alive, he was not conscious. Fresh tears streamed down Caine's cheeks as he hugged his brothers' hulking shoulders.

An agonizing scream echoed in the distance. He looked back to where he had slain the creature, Abigail. Her body was gone. All that remained was the knife lying on the ground. The Reapers were gone as well.

Caine gently plucked the large knife from the ground, inspecting the dull blade. Any attempt he had made to strike the girl's ghost had failed—all except for this strange, dull knife. Tucking the blade back into his belt and grabbing Ryler under his arms, he dragged the larger man across the remainder of purgatory, through the border, and into the land of the living. Once safely on the other side, Caine's last reserves of strength depleted, he dropped beside Ryler.

They were alive. They were alive, and he would ensure they stayed that way for as long as he could. Turning his head, he watched his brother's chest rise and fall steadily as he allowed slipped into the darkness of exhaustion that had been pursuing Caine since they first crossed the border into Purgatory.

The Gloomweaver's Gift

"I know this is hard for you, Lyanna, but I need you to tell me exactly what happened and how you felt. The more details you provide, the better."

The young woman across the table from me wrung her fingers together, wrinkling the delicate fabric of her thin gloves. Her distress was evident, causing the few patrons at the surrounding tables to stand and move to seats further away, tossing suspicious looks in our direction, primarily at me. Swiping at a few tears that had rolled down her cheeks, she nervously glanced about the room, no doubt noticing the attention we were gathering.

"Please, Sir. I don't understand what the details have to do with the… *job* that I am hiring you for. I was told that you could help me deal with the men who ra… um… hurt me. You are the…" She looked nervously about the establishment before leaning forward and lowering her voice. "You *are* The Gloomweaver, right?" Her lower lip trembled slightly.

I softened my voice and tried to take on as much of a sympathetic tone as possible. Despite my line of work, I sometimes struggled to get prospective clients to trust me. "Yes, I am. And I need these details to do my job to the best of my ability. By taking on the task of not only finding me but visiting me personally, you have shown me just how brave you have been throughout this entire ordeal. All I ask is for a little more bravery and cooperation."

Her eyes narrowed slightly, glancing up and down my person to likely judge my credibility. Despite my attempt to look as non-threatening as possible in a simple set of hiking trousers and a clean white shirt, there was only so much I could do with the scars lacing down my arms, across my face, and dotting what little bit of my chest was exposed by the laced neckline of my shirt. My long, black hair was even cleaned and pulled back into a simple knot. Despite my lean build, my stature was on the smaller side, thanks to my mother's tiny frame, and this at least aided in my attempt to come across as harmless to potential clients.

Coming to some decision, Lyanna nodded to herself, took a deep breath, and sat a little taller in her seat. Her voice was soft despite her resolution, and I had to lean slightly forward and strain to hear her.

"He was a large, overweight man. I met him in the market district about a month ago. He seemed nice enough and came across as very unassuming. He sold textiles, you see. And I am an avid seamstress for my Lady." She motioned to the well-crafted shawl she wore over her simple, long-sleeved servant dress to prove her point. The shawl was a creamy beige and was decorated with a thin stitching of blue doves around the hem.

"His prices were fair, and he was never anything but polite and respectful. After a few weeks of occasionally browsing and purchasing his goods whenever I was in the market, he asked to introduce me to a friend of his, one who sold thread of every color. Looking back now, I would have known if such a vendor had existed. Regardless, I agreed, and the man asked that I return at the end of the day and not forget to bring money for the threads."

Lyanna stopped then, taking a few short breaths and sniffling. Her apprehension was nearly palpable. Closing my eyes while she was distracted by her thoughts, I allowed the feeling to wash over me. A few moments later, Lyanna had calmed back down and continued.

"I asked my Lady that evening for an advance on my allowances. She has always been a wonderful Lady to be in service for and allowed me the advance. After I met with the man at his booth, which had been packed and closed, he led me away from the town center and into a smaller part of the city, toward the Southern District. Admittedly, I hadn't been there before and should have stopped and turned back or, at the very least, questioned where we were going. I began to have my doubts when we arrived. He let me inside a small hovel on a side street, where he introduced me to his friend. Then they... then..."

The young woman broke out into a full-on sob, attracting the attention of every patron left in the establishment. Avoiding the concerned and accusing glances in my direction, I moved my chair to sit beside hers, placing a gentle hand on her bowed back.

"I understand this is hard, but this is also the most important part. I promise that you will feel much better afterward. But, to do so, I need you to tell me everything in as much detail as possible. If you are uncomfortable, you can whisper the details to me."

I had learned the hard way a few years ago that asking a client who was the victim of rape into a private room was not the best practice. Usually, victims of this caliber preferred somewhere public with easy access to escape. While their sense of security certainly made them more willing to share their experiences, the public's attention usually made trying to calm an emotionally unstable individual significantly more awkward and difficult.

Nodding, Lyanna wiped the tears and snot from her face as discretely as possible. The next half hour was filled with her sob-ridden recount of the two men and the horrors they had inflicted upon her before relieving her of her belongings, including her advance pay from her Lady, and releasing her with threats and promises of what would happen, should she tell anyone. Her long-sleeved dress and thick shawl, usually reserved for winters and an odd wardrobe choice for the current hot season, made sudden sense.

Throughout her story, I allowed her emotions to overwhelm me. Terror, disgust, shame, hate, and remorse. Her story eventually came to a close.

"Thank you for telling me everything, Lyanna. Now, take a deep breath, as deep as you possibly can, and I promise you will feel better. Think about expelling every bad feeling into the world on the exhale. It sounds silly, but it will help."

At this point, Lyanna had tried to distance herself from me slightly on her chair. Unfortunately, I needed to be as close to her as possible for this part of the consultation. After eyeing me suspiciously, she finally closed her eyes and followed my instructions. On her long exhale, I closed my own eyes and felt the last of her anguish slip into the atmosphere around us. Her eyes flared open, elation blooming on her face. She grinned widely at me, showcasing perfectly straight teeth, before catching herself and clearing her throat, looking away to hide her embarrassment.

"Thank you, Sir. It is as you said. I feel much better now."

Returning her smile with one of my own, I stood from my chair and stepped back two paces to give her some sense of comfort.

"That is wonderful, and I am glad to hear it. With that, our consultation is complete. Please, do not waste another moment thinking about these men. They won't bother you or anyone else again. One last question before we go our separate ways, and perhaps I should have started with this. What was this man's name?"

"I wouldn't be surprised if it were fake, but he called himself Finnian. I didn't ask for his surname, I'm sorry. But here, as promised." She stood and placed a small linen bag of clinking coins on the table. I assumed by the quality alone that she must have made the bag by hand. "This amount hardly seems enough. I feel as though you have lifted the weight of an ox off my shoulders." Her straight-toothed smile broke free again.

Pocketing the small bag, I bowed slightly. "That is quite all right. Having been able to lift your burdens even the slightest bit would have been enough if I didn't have to pay for food and lodging. Have a good evening."

Leaving the small pub tucked between a smithy and a pottery shop, I stepped out into the warm, humid night. Despite the massive pressure on my chest and shoulders, one perhaps equal to the weight of an ox, I had to struggle to contain my delight. As grateful as I was that my client felt better after off-loading her emotions onto me, I loved my gift for what happened next.

Over the next two days, I managed to find the man Lyanna had fallen victim to. Not surprisingly, many merchants sold fabrics in such a large seaport city—her description of the portly man aided in my search. Putting eyes on the man alone caused the emotions I had gleaned from the woman to flare. Fighting back nausea, I struck up a conversation with the man. I fabricated a story that I thought might interest him, explaining that I was a foreigner to the city and looking for the best quality fabric and thread I could find before returning to my rural home.

I told the man that I had just taken on the position of my Baron's aide in my small providence and was sent to fetch quality wares from the port city to prepare for an upcoming ball. Finnian absorbed my act of an innocent and unassuming farmhand with little real-world experience as a starving man would a five-course meal. A sinister smile spread across his pockmarked face as he became more friendly and sympathetic to my cause. To seal this man's fate, I let him in on the secret that my Baron insisted the price was no issue and had given me more than would be realistically needed to procure the finest wares this city could offer.

Greed clouded Finnian's features as he excitedly claimed to know a friend in the city who sold the finest thread I could find, along with other quality items. Feigning excitement and gratitude, I agreed to meet the man again after the sun had receded and the market closed.

On the other side of the city, I stopped by the simple tavern on the docks where I had rented a room and retrieved a change of clothes in preparation for the night's rendezvous with my new friend. I exchanged my clean white shirt for a black long-sleeved tunic, covered by a thin leather vest and matching vambraces, each housing small blades. My everyday trousers were replaced with thick black leather that hugged my lower body, allowing easier movement. Lastly, I adorned my regular black boots and a thick black cloak to complete the ensemble and hide my clothing underneath. Miscellaneous gear I might find useful was hidden within multiple pouches lining the inside of my cloak.

Later that evening, I met with Finnian and was led to what I assumed was the same small hovel he had taken Lyanna. It was a wonder that the woman hadn't noticed all the signs that this was a trap. Regardless, I continued the act of a simpleton until I was brought inside the small building.

The smell of refuse and human filth immediately assaulted my nose. The next was the thick tobacco smoke that burned my eyes. Finnian introduced me to Aric, his supposed friend and fellow merchant. At the sound of the deadbolt behind me dropping into place, I struggled not to drop the act. Instead, I looked surprised at the obvious trap, glancing back and forth between the two men with faux fear reflected in my expression.

While Finnian was heavily overweight, Aric was equally thin. Quite a pair, these two were.

"Alright, boy, this is what's going to happen now." Finnian moved from behind me to stand next to Aric, who had brandished a small knife and pointed it in my direction. "You're gonna hand over all the coin you've got nice and easy, along with any weapons you might have hidden under that cloak of yours. After that, we're just gonna have some fun before sending you on your way. We don't want to have'ta hurt you, but we will if you put up a fight."

I frightened step backward, allowing a tremor into my voice. "What do you mean by 'fun?'"

Snickering, Aric grabbed the crotch of his pants, adjusting himself. "Don't you worry 'bout that part. I'll make sure you enjoy yourself, too."

31

Just as Finnian reached towards me, I dropped the act, my smile of delight finally making its appearance. As expected, both men recoiled slightly at my expression. I knew my smile, when not controlled, was disturbing. I had been told just as much by a few accomplices I occasionally worked with when a larger crew was needed. With my client's assailants only being two men past their middle-aged prime, this job I could carry out on my own.

"Now, let's get this started, shall we?" I reveled in the confusion flickering across their faces as I took control of the situation. "I'm looking forward to having a bit of fun of my own."

I loosened two small vials tied to the inside of my cloak. As they shattered on the rough stone floor, a thick blue mist exploded and quickly filled the room. Holding the corner of my cloak over my nose, I watched as the men crumpled to the floor in a fit of coughing and wheezing. As I waited for the mist to dissipate, I casually paced around the room, taking in my surroundings.

The only door to the establishment was to my back and conveniently locked, thanks to Finnian. At the far side of the room, a large table containing half-eaten bread and old bowls of what I hoped was stew stood with three crooked wooden chairs. A small hearth with a lit fire was placed in the wall to my left. Several metal utensils hung from a hook protruding from the wall beside the fire. On the right side of the room was a scattering of shelves, crates, and baskets, all containing miscellaneous odds and ends of little value. Most likely, these were the "goods" the men stole from their victims after assaulting them.

Once the air was safe to breathe, I got to work. Procuring

long, thin rope from my cloak, I hog-tied both men, ensuring their fists were tied closed, then I dragged them over to the hearth and placed them just in front of the fire so that I had the best lighting possible. The skinny man, Aric, began to get his wits about him first. His coughing finally subsided, and he stared back at me with wide eyes while struggling against his restraints.

"Wha'dya think your doin', boy? You best untie me now. Right now!" His voice broke on the last few words, discrediting his threat. I could almost feel his fear wafting from him in waves, sticky and pungent.

While waiting for Finnian's fit to subside, I pulled a chair from the table and sat before them. The fear and uncertainty from both men was palpable now. Rather than absorb it as I had with Lyanna, I slowly began releasing the woman's terror into the air. When only a fraction of the terror she felt had been released, Aric began shaking uncontrollably while the smell of urine and a growing puddle emerged from beneath Finnian.

I lowered my voice to its natural tenor and leaned back as leisurely as I could in the small, crooked chair, which was quite uncomfortable.

"Now that we are all settled, perhaps I should share why I am here tonight. I know you thought you had managed to snag yourself a good haul, luring a simple foreign man away from the city proper. I'm sure you would have stolen my coin and belongings, assaulted me, had your 'fun'..." My upper lip pulled back in disgust at the memory of Aric adjusting his crotch. "And then let me leave with threats and promises of retribution if I told so much as a soul what happened. Does that sound about right? Perhaps a typical night for you, gentlemen?"

As I spoke, I released more of Lyanna's terror until my reserve was nearing empty, and the men were all but sobbing messes on the ground. It was pathetic how two men could not handle between them the shared terror of one woman. Lyanna did not realize how strong she was to have been able to contain these emotions within herself without breaking apart entirely. I silently commended the woman while allowing her aggressors to wiggle helplessly in terror. It was only a few moments before both were begging and pleading, promising payment and goods in exchange for their release.

I leaned forward and propped my elbows on my knees, giving both men a stern look. "Now, don't tell me you're giving up already? The fun is only just beginning." The men stopped begging and watched with wide eyes, Aric sobbing silently. Standing, I leisurely stepped over the tied form of Finnian, enjoying the way he flinched away from me. Directly in front of the hearth, I grabbed two hanging metal utensils: a poorly made ladle and a chipped spatula. After a quick inspection of the items, I placed them both on the ledge before the fire so that the handles of both utensils lay in the flames. When the metal began to glow a cherry red, I grabbed the cooler end of the utensils with the corners of my cloak and turned back to the rapists on the floor.

"You must think yourselves such scary men. Luring unsuspecting simpletons into your trap to rob, assault, and rape them. Does that make you feel powerful?" Crouching down between the men, they both flinched away from the heat of the utensils burning in my grip. "You might think yourselves powerful, but I think you're both cowards. You don't even have the stomach to threaten your victims effectively. Here, let me show you a simple method you can use almost anywhere."

I grasped Finnian's tied wrists and slipped the ladle's molten hot handle between his bound fists so that it nestled tightly between his palms. The sizzling of skin and smell of burnt flesh was immediate, as were the portly man's screams. Writhing at my feet, he made feeble attempts to release the handle that was most likely already fusing to his skin.

While my back was turned, Aric had attempted to wiggle away. He had made it less than a couple of feet before I moved to him next. His round, freighted eyes tracked every movement of the spatula handle I still held aloft.

"Now, now. Don't be afraid. You're a big, scary man who preys on unsuspecting women, aren't you? Surely, holding a warm bit of metal isn't a big deal. After all, if you can stomach robbing and raping both men and women alike, surely you can stomach this."

I snatched his bound fists before he could get any further and slipped the burning metal between his palms. His agonized screams joined his partners.

Settling back in my chair, I watched the flames and waited for the men to calm down. Curses, screams, tears, and a few vomiting episodes later, both men quieted into a dazed silence.

Tapping the heel of my boot against the stone floor, a small blade slid from the tip of my toe. Shifting forward ever so slightly, I pressed the sharpened tip lightly into Finnian's throat. He stopped breathing as he snapped out of his daze. His eyes widened to an almost impressively round shape.

"I am just dying to know what goes through your mind when you lure unsuspecting innocents to this little home of yours." I hissed. "At first, I thought you were tough, scary men. But if touching a warm bit of metal is enough to reduce you to tears, perhaps I was mistaken. So, what's your excuse? Can't find a willing partner using your own merits, so you resort to trickery and force?"

"Look, it's not like we force them t' come along." Aric's words were a slur. "They walk down to this side o' the city on their own two legs." Aric swallowed so hard that there was an audible click. "If they aren't smart enough to turn back, then they deserve wha' they got comin'."

In all of the years I had under my belt dealing with criminals, murderers, and rapists alike, it never ceased to amaze me the convoluted rationalities people like the men before me could spew. A popular one was that women who dressed well and went out on the town for a good time were practically begging for a man to come along and assault them as if someone's choice of clothing was permission for rape.

I continued to stare in complete disappointment at the thin man. Under my unblinking gaze, he resumed his squirming. A surprised yelp from the fat man under the toe of my boot stopped his friend's movements. Blood began to stream from the small cut in the fat of Finnian's neck.

"So let me get this right. If a harmless woman, or man for that matter, were to trust you and follow you down the city, then they *deserve* to be robbed, assaulted, raped, and threatened? Is that right?"

Before either of them could find the courage to respond, I released the entirety of Lyanna's shame. Although she felt shame for a very different reason, it was the emotion that was released, not the reasoning behind it.

This was where the finesse of my job came in. To convince my subjects to feel the emotions in the way that I want them to, I have to lead their thoughts and emotions in the right direction before adding to them. Emotions such as shame and remorse were especially difficult, as it took at least a sliver of the subject's matching feelings to exist before I could escalate it with the one I released. I also have to ensure their thoughts are on the right topic.

For example, suppose I pass a man on the street who I had seen earlier kick a dog. In that case, I have to remind him of the dog before releasing remorse, or he will instead associate the emotion with whatever was most recently on his mind.

Much to my satisfaction, I watched as the shame took hold in both men. Aric bowed his head, allowing it to thump onto the stone floor. Finnian closed his eyes, and tears sprang anew, running down the sides of his face and into his greasy hairline. The smell of burnt flesh was so strong that my own eyes threatened to water.

"Now, I am sure that neither of you have any children, or at least none that you are aware of." I glared at each of them and released a fraction of the remorse I had stored up. "However, for the sake of this lesson, imagine you had wives and daughters. If they followed a merchant who claimed to have the wares they were searching for to an establishment and then *raped* them, could you reasonably say that the fault lay with the women? Imagine the shame they would feel coming back home to you. Think of the terror they must feel ever going out into public again. And you truly feel this is justified?"

I allowed the rest of the remorse I had stored to seep out into the air of the room. Both men's sobs filled the silence, Finnian shaking so severely that the blade in the toe of my boot drew fresh blood. He didn't even notice, and I didn't care enough to ease the pressure.

"How many lives have you ruined, I wonder?" Slowly and carefully, as this was the most challenging emotion to release with the intended result, I let slip hate. Finnian's sobs took on an impressive intensity while Aric's ceased altogether. Instead, he began slamming his head against the hard stone floor. His eyes screwed shut as pain and inner turmoil undoubtedly roiled within him.

I allowed the men to stew in their heightened emotions for a few minutes longer before abruptly standing. Both men's gazes snapped to mine.

"Now then, I believe I have gotten my point across." Standing between the men, I crouched down to as near eye level as possible. "If at any point I hear about any more men or women being robbed, assaulted, or even touched inappropriately, even if it wasn't by your hands, I will be back. And believe me..." I quickly reached down, seizing each man by the neck and releasing the mechanism holding my arm blades in place. Each man shouted in alarm as the tips of the blades dug into their flesh, deep enough to bleed but not enough to cause any permanent harm. "If I have to come back and waste any more breath talking to you two, I will ensure you live just long enough to regret it before doing this city a favor and ridding it of some of its filth."

After allowing the threat to sink in a moment longer, I released the last of my stored terror. I released the men, replaced the blades in my vambraces, and made my way to the door. I didn't bother to untie either man or remove the melted utensils from their flesh. Unhooking the latch and stepping out into the warm night air, I couldn't help but take a deep breath.

It felt like the weight of an ox had been removed from my shoulders.

Shatter

T he door was heavy, the metal surface painfully cold to the touch. Using all the strength I could muster, I managed to spin the wheel in the center of the door until I heard a loud, satisfying clink of the lock releasing. Putting my shoulder against the door, I pushed. The groaning of the hinges echoed in the emptiness around me, possibly used for the first time in an unknown amount of time.

Beyond the door, the air smelled stagnant, and a warm, humid breeze wafted through the open doorway. I glanced at my two companions behind me, receiving an encouraging nod. One by one, we stepped through the doorway into this new world.

It took a moment for my eyes to adjust to the darkness we had stepped into. Four stone walls led into a short corridor, housing a single door at the far end. The air in the corridor was warm and oppressive.

The door at the end of the corridor didn't look as large or heavy as the one I had just pushed through, much to my relief. Making our way through the short enclosure and taking in our minimal surroundings, I felt tingling on the back of my neck. Something wasn't right. I looked again to my two companions following behind for any reaction, but neither seemed to feel the same eerie sense as I did. Deciding not to voice my concerns, I reached the next door and pushed it open on rusted hinges.

We emerged into an old abandoned subway system, stepping onto a large platform that ended at what may have once been tracks, though rubble and darkness hid what lay below. In either direction, the tunnel disappeared into the darkness. Only a narrow walkway on the side of the tunnel allowed access down each path. Looking into the seemingly endless tunnels, a chill ran down my back, the same sense of dread from earlier amplifying. Hoping to reach the surface, I headed up a wide set of stairs alongside my two companions.

Brought together by some unknown force, I have spent the past few months traveling with two others on countless worlds through numerous doors, trying to find either our way home or the reason behind our abductions and the roles we were meant to play.

Though we come from entirely different worlds, we grew close during our travels. Closest behind me was Rue. Her thick, curly, sandstone-colored hair was tied back in a messy ponytail. Her face, as usual, lacked any emotion that she might have felt, whereas I was sure that mine easily portrayed my unease. Her face was dirty, as were her clothes, from constant traveling with little opportunity to bathe. Minor scrapes and bruises dotted her smooth brown skin. Despite the evidence of our travels, she was still beautiful. From her almond-shaped eyes to the graceful way she carried herself, she reminded me of elves from the fairy tales I had read as a child.

Behind Rue came Tairman, always guarding the rear of our small group. He didn't look much better when it came to wear, his short black hair having grown long enough to lay in different directions. We had tried many times to tie the unruly locks back into a band, but the thick strands of hair refused to be tamed. He was also covered in small wounds, though his pale skin tended to bruise more easily than mine or Rue's. Noticing my gaze, he gave me a reassuring smile, his unnaturally bright blue eyes shining with support. No matter the circumstances we managed to find ourselves in, he always found a way to make light of the situation. I wanted to ask if he felt the same unnerving feeling as I did, but it didn't feel right to shatter the silence that had gone unbroken since our arrival.

Reaching the top of the long stairwell, we were confronted with yet another door. This one looked large and heavy, like the first we had passed through. I muscled the wheel to unlock it and pushed the heavy door outward. After hours in the darkness, intense sunlight blinded me, forcing me to shield my eyes. After a few moments of blinking and squinting, I took in my new surroundings as my vision refocused.

We were finally outside, and I felt momentary relief at being out of the confining underground passageways. Ahead of me stretched a large walkway about twenty feet across, made of individual red-clay bricks. On either side of the walkway stood tall brick walls double my height, limiting my view of what might be beyond.

All I could see above the walls were the distant tops of buildings and spires. The world lacked color, as if I were viewing it through a beige filter. Despite the blinding sun that seemed uncomfortably close, the air was cool. The bricks lining the pathway and walls were covered in scorch marks. The tops of the buildings I could see over the walls looked little more than giant skeletons, as though they had been slowly crumbling for decades.

I glanced behind me at Rue and Tairman, only to find that I stood alone on the walkway. The door we had just come through was closed, even though I had neither closed it nor heard it being shut. Panic overtook me as I scrambled to remove a small radio from the pack on my back. My companions carried similar packs, which had appeared with us when we were first brought together. I called on the radio for them and received only static in return. A sick ball of panic gripped my stomach, and I prayed they were safe.

After a few seconds that felt like hours, they finally responded. Lightheaded with relief, I nearly sank to my knees as my strength waivered. None of us understood what happened or how we were separated, but they reported the same observations as I did. With the looming walls around us and the closed underground behind, it seemed there was only one direction left to go: forward. We could only hope that our paths converged again at some point down this pathway.

Taking a deep breath, I shouldered my pack and started down the pathway. I had only been walking for a few minutes when a faint sound stopped me. Holding my breath, I strained to listen, rewarded by ringing silence. I realized then that the decaying city surrounding me was as silent as death. After a moment more of straining to hear, I resumed walking.

A reasonable distance down the walkway, I came upon a massive tower. Lost in my thoughts, I hadn't noticed the structure until a deep thrumming brought me back to the present. Despite how old and destroyed the buildings on the other side of the wall looked, the tower that loomed before me seemed recent. Its structure reminded me of the large electrical towers that ran lines between cities when I was a child, yet there were no wires or cords that I could see. The legs of the structure connected to the tops of the walls on either side of the pathway ahead of me. As I ventured nearer, the deep thrumming I felt before turned into a buzzing sound, reminding me of the hum of electricity. Walking directly beneath the structure was the only way to get past it.

As I took my first step under the structure, I felt like gravity had suddenly strengthened. I could feel my body being pulled downward as each step became more difficult, like trudging through molasses. Unable to process what was happening, I considered turning back. However, turning back would only return me to the starting point. Panic threatened to grip me again, but I pushed it down. Taking as deep of a breath as I could, I continued.

Each step grew heavier, and each breath became harder. Just past the halfway point under the structure, I was forced to my hands and knees and reduced to crawling. My breaths came in short, labored gasps. On hands and knees, I crawled on.

As I finally neared the end of the structure, my skin felt as if it was being pulled down to the ground, threatening to tear from my very bones. Despite the forces working against me, I finally pulled myself past the final support leg of the tower, crawling on my belly. Instantly, the weight lifted. Fresh air raced into my lungs as I lay there, gasping. With the sudden release of pressure, I felt lighter than ever. The sudden weightlessness, accompanied by panic racing through my veins, gave me the strength to jump back to my feet and pick up the pace. I was happy to put distance between myself and the buzzing tower.

I walked for what felt like hours, though it might only been minutes. Time seemed to stand still in this realm, as the sun never moved from its position directly above me. Occasionally,

I tried radioing my group to make sure they were alright, curious if they had run into any obstacles as I had. The only response I received was static. After a fourth attempt at contact, I accepted that I was alone for the moment, returned the radio to my pack, and trudged on.

For a long while, I only heard the scuffing of my boots against the path and my labored breathing. The faint whisper of a sound made me pause. I held my breath and strained to listen. It was similar to the sound I had heard before the tower. The cold lump of dread in my stomach grew as I stood still, listening.

Stepping slowly and lightly, I continued forward. Glancing left to right, I was greeted with the same view of tall brick walls and distant crumbling buildings beyond. Once more, I heard the sound. Movement at the edge of my vision caught my attention, and I whirled to my left. Nothing was there but the ever-present, looming wall. A chill ran down my back as I started walking again, nearly at a jog now. Again, I heard it, this time close enough for me not to doubt my sanity. The hissing noise reminded me of a whisper, but I couldn't fathom any words.

I came to a dead stop as I approached another bend in the pathway, despair making my limbs heavy. Looming before me was another tower that buzzed with the same electrical hum as the last one. I was given no time to decide what to do before the hissing whisper motivated me to press on and get to the end of the path, wherever it may lead. Much to my dismay, the gravity around this tower was the same as the last.

I felt as though I was being pulled into the ground as I struggled to make it pass. As I did with the last, I made it to the other side just before I felt I could no longer go on. The sudden relief of pressure made me feel lighter than ever. I jumped to my feet and continued onward in a sprint.

The further I ran, the closer the whispering voice seemed to get. No matter how many times I whirled left and right, trying to catch a glimpse of the sound's source, it managed to stay on the outskirts of my peripherals. Panic spurred me onward as my breathing came in haggard gasps. I came upon another tower. And then another, and another. Tears stung at the corner of my eyes, threatening to fall as terror threatened to take over the last of my reason. The whispers sounded as if they were right behind me, but I knew that if I stopped to look, I would lose the strength to move forward.

Just as hopelessness began to envelop me, I saw the end. The pathway abruptly ended with another large metal door. Unlike before, the door was open. Without a second thought, I darted through the door frame and put all my weight behind me, shutting the dying world out with a deafening bang. Engulfed in sudden darkness, more blinding than the sunlight, I heard only my labored breathing and my heart threatening to burst from my chest. I had no idea if I had just reached salvation or my end by shutting myself in. However, I no longer heard the inhuman whispering, which was good enough for me.

When I finally caught my breath and my eyes adjusted to the darkness, I stood at the top of a large stairwell, not unlike the one my companions and I had ascended when we first arrived. Taking another deep breath, I pushed off of the door and started down the stairs. At the bottom, my knees went weak at the sight of Rue and Tairman. They stood with their backs to me, heads close together to exchange whispered words. When they spotted me, smiles broke free, and we embraced. Tears of relief streamed down my cheeks.

I asked about the towers, the noises I had heard outside, and if they had experienced the same. My questions were met with confusion. They had not heard any noises nor passed by any of the gravitational structures as I had. After we were separated, they had only walked a short distance down a similar pathway before reaching another door leading them back underground. They had arrived only moments before I did, despite my journey feeling like it lasted the better part of a day.

Not for the first time, an overwhelming wrongness pushed down upon me, and all I wanted to do was move on from this world. It took little convincing before the three of us set off once again. This underground system of subway tunnels was uncomfortably similar to the one we had arrived in. However, when we reached the end of the hallway, which should have ended with the single metal door we had entered through, three stood instead. Each looked the same, though I felt they were significantly different. An odd compulsion led me to the middle door, whereas Rue and Tairman were each convinced we should enter through one of the side doors. After a quick discussion, we decided that each of us should open a door simultaneously.

As I turned the large wheel in the center door, the sickness of terror and dread gripped me again as I heard the whispering. This time, the sound was coming from the other side of the door. I stood helpless as the door swung open. Before me loomed a figure reminiscent of a young woman wearing a dirty white nightgown. The garment was torn and shredded, barely hanging from the woman's atrophied frame. Her long, grey hair looked greasy, the unkempt locks falling well past her shoulders. As disturbing as the entirety of her figure was, her face, or lack thereof, made my blood freeze.

Where features should have been, instead was a twisting hole. As I stared into the swirling nothingness of her face, pain flared in my chest. I nearly fell to my knees, grabbing the door for support. A shrill scream filled my head, bringing forth a scream of my own. I pushed the massive door shut, closing myself off from the creature and subsequently ending the pain in my chest. Turning, I ran into the arms of Rue and Tairman, the two of them having abandoned their doors to rush to my side.

I fell to my knees before them, explaining through clattering teeth what I had seen. They shared a concerned glance before telling me that they had neither seen nor heard anything other than my terrified scream. Rue knelt beside me and put a reassuring hand on my shoulder. Despite her emotionless gaze, I realized they must think I was insane.

I was unprepared for the uncontrollable weeping that took over me. Shivers racked my body, my teeth chattering painfully. Rue and Tairman tried to comfort me as I cried, reassuring me that everything would be alright. Their words hardly reached me, the memory of the figure flashing before me every time I closed my eyes, her shrill scream lingering in my mind. Despite their attempts to calm me, I only wept harder.

Finally, they managed to lift me to my feet. I wiped the tears from my eyes and tried to inhale. Terrified or not, we had to leave this place. I turned to look at the other two doors, the question of which we should try beginning to form on my lips. The words died before I could utter them, for within inches from me stood the tormented figure. Her scream echoed in my head, and I felt my mind shatter.

Ashes of Innocence

Deep within the recesses of the Bardourn Mountains, a small village with no name lay nestled between three of the highest peaks. So cut off from the rest of the world, neither existed to the other. Late one autumn, a boy was born in this nameless village to a family of wheat farmers. As was tradition for the firstborn son, he took on the name of his great-grandfather on his paternal side of the family. Richart. It was a good name, a strong name.

Richart spent the first few years of his life as any boy might. He had a mother who doted on him, a father who taught him how to farm and provide for a family, and an older sister whom he loved dearly, regardless of how much they fought. The world, to Richart, was vast with endless possibilities. He was friends with the other young boys, spent the early mornings learning how to farm with his father, afternoons helping his mother with chores, and evenings exploring the small town and surrounding forest with his friends. His world was vast, comfortable, and more than he could ever ask for.

His world ended three nights before he would celebrate his sixth autumn.

~*~

Richart woke with a start. Cool air billowed through the open window curtains in the bedroom he shared with his older sister, Janneth. He strained to listen, curious about what had woken him. He heard only silence; not even the sound of crickets or frogs. He felt something was wrong but didn't know what it could be. He didn't think he had forgotten any of his chores; he wouldn't have been allowed supper if he had.

He lay there in silence, listening to Janneth's quiet snores from her bed a few feet away. He could hear the sawing sound of his father's snoring through the wall. His mother always teased him for it, saying that his father dreamed of sawing down trees in his sleep, and his snores were the sounds of the many toothed blades against tree trunks. Try as he might, he couldn't fall back to sleep. He breathed deeply and squeezed his eyes shut. He even tried counting hay bales, as his father had taught him. Nothing seemed to work. Quietly, so as not to wake Janneth, he crept out of his bed, across their small room, and into the kitchen.

Without the sound of his family's snores, the quiet felt unnatural. Richart headed to a large clay jug that sat next to the hearth, the rim of which came up to his chest. He grabbed a spoon hanging from a nail by the dying fire and dipped it into the jug, only to come up dry. Standing on the tips of his toes, he peered into its depths. It was nearly empty, and he was not quite tall enough to reach the water at the bottom. He considered returning to bed but knew he would only lay awake. A sudden idea gripped him, and he grinned. Uneasiness forgotten and replaced by excitement. He grabbed a bucket that sat by the door and stepped out into the night air.

Hurrying through the quiet roads leading to the center of town, he thought of how happy Ma and Pa would be when they woke to find that he had fetched water all by himself. A toothy grin slid across his face. He was always told to stay away from the town well since he was too small to reach the rope in the middle, but he had grown quite a bit over the past summer. But he was bigger now, almost as tall as his father's belly.

"A man's pride is providing for his family." Pa would always say whenever Richart asked why he stayed out past sundown working in the fields. He wanted to be a man like Pa and prove he could provide for his family.

Just before he reached the well at the town's center, Richart stopped. Something still didn't seem right. It wasn't odd that the streets were empty; It was very deep into the night. Even the animals had all gone to bed. That was when Richart realized what was strange: the nighttime creatures were not singing their songs. He had noticed this earlier when he first woke but hadn't thought too deeply about how odd that was. The woods that nearly swallowed the village had never been so quiet in all the years he could remember. Trying to ignore the eerie feeling, he approached the round brick wall surrounding the deep well.

Across the top of the well's opening sat a wooden and metal structure that housed a long coil of rope ending with a hook hovering directly over the center of the well. His father told him it was called a 'pulley,' which Richart remembered because it seemed like such a silly word, one a baby might use when speaking gibberish. He had watched dozens of people pull buckets of water from the well and was confident he could do it. He just had to hook the rope handle of the bucket, untie the rope from where a stake in the ground secured it, lower the bucket, and then bring it back up. It was that simple!

The brick wall surrounding the well's entrance came up to his chest, which meant he had to pull himself up to the ledge to reach the hook. Reaching, the tips of his fingers brushed the hook, causing it to sway away from him. He grumbled as he stretched out and tried again, smacking the hook with his palm instead of grabbing it. It swung away, and he caught it on the swing back. Triumphant, he hopped back down from the wall.

Richart draped the rope handle of the bucket across the metal hoop and released it so that it swung free over the mouth of the well. His hands nearly shook with excitement as he untied the anchor and lowered the bucket. The well was much deeper than he had imagined, and it took quite a while before he heard a small splash and saw the rope go slack. He pulled the rope to bring it back up and nearly stumbled into the wall! He hadn't expected the full bucket to be so heavy. Hand over hand and heaving with all his might, he took nearly ten minutes to bring the bucket back up, pausing several times to catch his breath and nurse the blisters forming on his hands from the rope. Tears pricked at the corners of his eyes, but he blinked them away.

I'm going to be a man soon, just like Pa. And Pa never cries! Determined, he worked the rope and pulley until the sloshing bucket sat firmly below the contraption and the rope was again anchored.

As he again climbed onto the wall of the well, he looked down into the inky depths, wondering how far down the water's surface was. The full moon high above provided ample light, but the well was so deep that he couldn't see all the way down. His limbs froze as fear raced through him. The bucket swayed heavily a few feet before him, well within arm's reach. But with the gaping maw of darkness just below him, those few feet felt like miles.

Maybe I'm still not big enough to fetch water from the well without help, he thought.

A loud, roaring noise filled the silent night. The sound was so sudden and out of place that Richart flinched, which caused him to lose his grip on the wooden structure. His knees slipped off the wall's ledge, and he plummeted into darkness. He was submerged in cold water before he could process what had happened. Panic and adrenaline filled his limbs as he kicked and clawed at nothing, trying to reach the water's surface. He couldn't tell which way was up or down between the darkness and the lingering disorientation of his fall.

Somehow, he managed to break the water's surface, gasping and coughing up water. Looking up toward the entrance to the well, he could barely make out the night sky far above his head. Stars and the moon's edge were only visible from a small circle far above his head. Clinging to the clay and mud-slicked wall, he shouted for help. His shouts were drowned out by another terrifying roar, sounding closer than before. Richart trembled as the rumbling from the sound could be felt in his bones. Before he could shout again, a single, high-pitched scream cut him short.

Everything seemed to happen all at once. Richart had no idea what was happening from down the well, but he could no longer see the night sky through the opening far above him. Instead, he saw fire. The flames were so intense that they illuminated his watery prison. Blinded, Richart covered his eyes, causing him to fall from the small perch he had been clinging to and diving under the water again.

Breaking the water's surface and gasping for air, Richart

tried to scream with all his might for help while grabbing at the walls around him. Far above, chaos had erupted. He could hear men and women alike screaming and shouting and an occasional thundering sound that sent chills down to his core.

Richart finally succumbed to the sobs that had been threatening him since he fell. He was cold, scared, confused, and had no idea what was happening. Somehow, he felt it was his fault for disobeying his Ma by leaving the house at night and trying to pull for water. Maybe this was his punishment. His choking sobs were only interrupted by the clacking of his teeth by the force of his shivers.

Another wave of fire passed over the well. This time, Richart looked away from the surface so as not to be blinded again. Looking back just as the fire disappeared, he saw his way out. Spiraling up the sides of the well were displaced bricks. They only stuck out of the clay and mud surface by a few inches, but that was enough for Richart to find purchase with his small hands and feet.

Hope welled in his chest as he began to climb. After he had climbed a few feet above the surface of the water, something fell past him, narrowly missing him before it splashed in the water. Turning to look over his shoulder, he was nearly hit again as a bucket full of water was pulled back to the surface. Then another bucket dropped, and another.

Richart began climbing even faster. His body shook, his limbs ached, and his head pounded. Yet he continued to climb until he was nearly at the surface of the well. He could no longer feel his hands or feet, only the numbing cold from his time in the depths and the intense heat from just outside the well. The buckets had stopped falling, and Richart could pull himself over the wall and onto the dirt on the other side.

Panting and clutching his chest, he rested against the wall.

The first thing he noticed was the silence. He had expected to see the villagers running around, screaming and yelling. Instead, he saw no one. The night was lit ablaze by the houses around him, either on fire or already burnt to the ground. A horrible stench filled the air, and he gagged as he gasped for breath. The smell reminded him of when he had gone to the blacksmith's workshop with his father and had touched a metal rod recently heated from the forge. The pain was unbearable, and the smell that came from his skin was similar to what he smelled now.

"Ma?" His voice was weak, and he couldn't stop shaking, even though he was no longer cold. "Pa?" He expected his mother to appear beside him, scolding him for disobeying her. But she didn't appear. No one did. Richart felt like he was the only person left in the world.

How had the fires started? He hadn't noticed anything when he left home. And what was it that had made those terrifying sounds?

As if summoned, he heard the sound again, this time much louder and closer than ever. It was hard to see past the billowing smoke from the fires. Richart longed to jump up, run home, and dive beneath the safety of his covers, but his body wouldn't respond to his demands. Instead, he sat helplessly against the wall of the well, steam rising from his damp clothes.

From the darkness behind the flames, something rose into the light.

Richart had never seen a creature like this before. It towered over the houses, making him feel like an ant in comparison. Its hide was covered in dark scales that reflected the dancing flames. Atop its massive head were rows of spikes longer than any knife Richart had ever seen.

He wanted to scream and run, but his body still refused to move. All he managed was a frightened squeal, which he immediately regretted. He slapped his hands over his mouth, barely leaving enough room between his fingers to breathe, but it was too late. The creature's massive head swung around to face him.

Moving faster than Richart would think a creature of that size should be capable of, it approached him. Its massive claws crushed what was left of the structures in its path without even seeming to notice. The steps that landed on the road left massive pits behind in the shape of its taloned feet. As the creature came into the clearing by the well, it opened its massive jowls, revealing rows of gigantic, pearly-white teeth stained with red. A foul stench washed over him from its hot breath. Richart involuntarily gagged.

Richart begged his body to move, to get up and run for his life, but he was frozen to the spot. He stared wide-eyed and unmoving as the black mass of scales and teeth came for him. The beast stopped just as Richart took what he thought would be his final breath. It paused for a few heartbeats before snapping its massive mouth shut and turning its head to peer at Richart with one giant eye.

The glassy orb was as round as Richart was tall. He saw himself reflected, and it reminded him of a cat's gaze with the large black pupil slicing down through the center of a field of yellow. Streaks of red shot away from the black pupil, the color forking like lightning. Despite how terrible the beast was, he couldn't help but admire the beauty of its eye. It watched him as he struggled to continue breathing. As terrified as he was, Richart couldn't bring himself to look away.

It felt like an eternity that he stared into the eye of the beast. Another roar from farther away broke the silence and broke the spell that held Richart in place. He pulled his knees to his chest and curled into a tight ball. Unable to resist, he shifted his arms to peek through the gap between them.

The massive eye still watched him. It blinked once before rising back up. Massive wings sprouted from its dark, scaly back. The size of its wingspan was so large that it made the hulking creature itself seem small. With one mighty beat of its bat-like wings, it was gone. The down draft flattened a few crumbling buildings and coated Richart in dirt and hot ashes.

He didn't know how long he sat there after the animal had left. Perhaps animal was not the right word, for it seemed much too intelligent for such a mundane description. After a time, he finally unfolded himself and stood on shaking legs. He stumbled between blazing structures and crumbling houses to his family's home. Or at least he returned to where his family's home *should* have been. Only charred remains greeted him.

Richart felt like he was in a terrible dream as he walked into what should have been the common room. Only ashes and burnt remains were left. His parents and sister were nowhere to be seen. He hoped they had managed to escape.

Stepping through the rubble, he went to his shared room where his bed used to be. Oh, how he longed to crawl underneath his worn and familiar covers. Regret and hopelessness flooded Richart as he fell to the ground, sobbing. Crawling to where Janneth's bed should be, he slumped down next to what remained of her bed frame.

What was he going to do now? How could he care for himself if he could not do something as simple as fetch a bucket of water? Where did those monsters come from, and why did they destroy everything? One question kept arising above all the rest. Why was he the only one spared?

Distant Hearts

Her name was Elenore Devonte. Classy, regal, civilized, and the epitome of the 1950s upper class with an attitude to match. Even at 96 years old, the woman was sharper than the needles of a porcupine and just as likely to go on the defensive and show her quills. The prickly woman had gone through several nurses before I was assigned as her caretaker at the retirement home where I worked. I would be lying if I said I hadn't considered putting in my request to transfer the client to another caretaker. The old crone reacted to my every sweet attempt at care just as well as a temperamental cat reacted to water.

After three months of any and all attempts to make peace with the woman, I had all but given up. In a last-ditch effort, I decided to change tactics. Rather than treat her with the same overly sensitive and agreeable attitude we normally used with our most elderly patients, I instead treated her as I would a frustrating colleague whom I had no choice but to work with.

Gone were my soft knocks at the door and gentle urges for the ancient woman to take her medicine. I no longer pleaded sweetly for her to allow me to assist her around her room or for a stroll on the premises. Although I may have donned a more aggressive approach to the woman's care, that does not mean I didn't show her the respect she deserved as my elder.

Shortly after changing my attitude around the woman, I noticed an immediate change in her demeanor, and our interactions became more comfortable. Rather than wave away any attempts I made to help her, she hesitantly let me assist her. The contemptuous glances were replaced with curiosity and, eventually, fondness. In a few short months, the woman's porcupine quills began to flatten, and I was allowed to see a side of her no one else had.

As it turns out, Elenore was simply tired of being treated like a child, though she was nearly three times older than any of her nurses. By treating her as I would any other person and not like a senile old woman, I had gained the woman's respect, much to the awe of my coworkers and the bafflement of her previous nurses.

Even into her late 90s, Elenore was as quick-witted and intelligent as any middle-aged woman I knew, with the memory befitting her life's work as an educator. Having lived through nine decades, the woman was full of experience and stories, from being born into a New York Mafia family in 1925 to attending Columbia University as a young woman, to meeting and falling in love with a foreign exchange student who turned out to be a young Arabian prince. I could never decide if I believed all of her stories, some seeming too fantastical to be real. Regardless, the story of her short-lived and forbidden love was beautiful, if not tragic, whether or not it was real.

As one of the top students in her Freshman class, Elenore had been assigned to assist their newest foreign exchange student in adjusting to campus life and ensuring he knew his way around. With so much time spent together, they quickly grew attached. He revealed to her his royal lineage, which she understandably did not believe at first. Her family stepped in as their time spent together increased, and their relationship became apparent. Blinded by prejudice, they took it upon themselves to warn the young prince to stay away from her.

Try as they might, they could not stay away from each other and continued to meet secretly. This continued for two years before they were exposed, and the prince was forced to return to Arabia.

Elenore stated that she could never love another as she had loved her prince. Refusing to open her heart again, she remained unmarried and without children for the entirety of her life.

Although I knew she had never married or had children of her own, I never knew that she had no surviving relatives at all until she passed in the summer of 2021, two years ago. Even her passing was elegant, simply retiring for the evening in her brand-name silk pajamas, only not to wake the following morning. As heartbreaking and shocking as the event was, an even bigger shock was that the woman had left all of her worldly possessions to none other than her caretaker. Me.

The late Elenore had, in fact, been born to a wealthy mafia family. As the only surviving heir and having none of her own, her family home was passed to me. A three-story, manor-style house on the outskirts of New York. The estate had been completely paid off decades ago, but I couldn't bring myself to sell the house or furnishings.

Honoring Elenore's memory, I packed up, moved out of my small 700-square-foot studio apartment in the city, and took up residence in the Devonte Manor, as I had taken to calling it. I would be lying if I said the large, nearly empty estate sometimes didn't spook me. However, over the next two years, I had come to love the place.

Even though I now had proof that a few more of Elenore's stories were true, such as her ties to the old mafia families, I still didn't quite believe them all, including the one about her long-lost prince. That all changed when the letter arrived.

The envelope had nearly been overlooked in my pile of junk mail and a few utility bills. What caught my attention was the sheer number of stamps covering the front. Elegant handwriting was addressed to a "Miss Elenore Devonte." The oldest date I could read on the first row of stamps was from 1947.

The letter was from someone named Amin Farid, but there was no return address.

I have always prided myself on being a law-abiding citizen of New York. I always throw my trash and recycling away in the correct receptacles. I only cross the street when the "WALK" light is illuminated. And never have I ever opened someone else's mail. But what do you do when the person addressed in the envelope is deceased and has no living relatives? With evidence of how well-traveled this letter was, I couldn't bring myself to throw it away when it had finally reached its destination.

Leaving the letter on the small breakfast table in the kitchen, I decided that this was a problem for later and instead busy myself with the dishes that I had let pile up over the past two days. There weren't many dishes to wash, and I soon ended up back in front of that letter.

What would happen if I opened it? Would anyone even know? Would it still be considered an invasion of privacy if the person whose privacy I was invading was deceased?

Conflicted, I remembered leaving laundry in the dryer before leaving for the nursing home that morning.

Two loads of laundry, a vacuumed and mopped kitchen, and a tidied manor later, I once again stood before the letter in the kitchen.

Flipping the envelope over, I noticed that the corner of the seal had already been torn. This proved the quality of the letter's stationery if this was the only damage it received after over 70 years of being passed around in the postal system between numerous countries. My fingers ached to grab the corner and finish tearing the envelope open. Who would know?

I suddenly needed to know now more than ever if the story of Elenore's mysterious Arabian Prince was true. This was no longer some whimsical curiosity but a burning desire to know the truth. A truth that was within my grasp, quite literally.

Sending a silent apology to the spirit of Elenore, I tore open the envelope. From it, I removed three sheets of aged paper. The texture of the parchment was thick and expensive, unlike anything I might receive in the mail nowadays. Whoever wrote the letter did so with an elegant, looping script. I treated the pages as delicately as glass and carried them to the nearest sitting room.

There were three sitting rooms in the manor, one on each floor. This room was perhaps my favorite in the entire estate. Located towards the back of the first floor and just behind the kitchen, the room was decorated in deep hues of blue, with beige accents and elegant crown molding. Three of the four walls were covered in shelves of books and near-ancient decorations. Despite the quality of the furnishings, this room was far from the most elegant. It was also one of the smallest, making it feel cozy.

Settling into my favorite oversized chair and cuddling under a thick quilt matching the room's theme, I began to read.

"My dearest Elenore,

I pray that this letter reaches you. Since we were separated, I have spent nearly every moment thinking of you and of how we were forced apart. There were so many words left unsaid, so many experiences I hoped we could have together, and I pray that somehow, we might still.

Even with the distance between us, I often find my thoughts wandering back to the nights we spent together, hand-in-hand, with no purpose in mind other than to be near one another. I can still hear your laughter and feel your hand in mine. The absence of you by my side has left a hole in my chest that cannot be filled by another.

I am not above admitting that coming to the United States was a terrifying experience. Our nations had only recently become friendly, and I felt alone. I had expected to visit your country to glean knowledge of your culture and economics. I never imagined I might find love as well.

Even after learning of my official status, you never treated me as anything more than just a man; a man that I hope one day will be worthy of your affections.

I understand the precarious position my title has put you in with your family dynamics. Had I ever stopped to think of the repercussions my attention and love would cause you... I wish I could say that I would have done things differently, but I cannot say with confidence that I would have. To not have experienced your love would have been as to never experience the brilliance of the sunrise after a long, dark night..."

The following two and a half pages were poetic professions

of his undying love for Elenore that no force could come between, not even that of his title or her family's profession. The writing was elegant, the words full of heartbreaking emotion.

The last few paragraphs were what brought me to tears.

"This will be forward of me, and I can only pray that you will forgive my presumptuousness. Please understand that this request comes from weeks of torment and contemplation. My love, I cannot be without you. My family and title demand that I wed to a woman of good standing, which limits my choices in the matter. However, though you are from a different nationality, I have been given my family's blessing to request your hand in marriage.

I know our time together was brief, and there is much of each other we did not have the time or opportunity to learn. I ask that you give me that opportunity now. Come to Arabia, my love, and be my wife. I understand the position this will put you in with your family, and I can promise that I will leverage every power I possess to prove to your family that I am deserving of your love.

I eagerly await your response, my love, for my life cannot continue without you by my side.

Forever yours, Amin."

Processing the entirety of the letter in my hands, my heart felt heavy. It was all true. Not only had Elenore met an Arabian prince and fallen in love, but he was so smitten with her that he convinced the royal family to accept her and make her his wife. Elenore had never known because the letter I now held in my hand had never reached her. I wonder now if that was why she had refused to leave this massive home until she could no longer care for herself. My heart broke further as I realized that by never responding to this declaration of love, the prince must have believed she had refused his proposal.

Hopping to my feet, I rushed to my room and opened my laptop. Being royalty, surely there had to be information on this prince. After some digging, I finally found the information I was looking for… in his eulogy. Amin Farid had indeed been a prince in Arabia. Born to a family of six siblings, he was the youngest and, in turn, held the least amount of responsibility and expectation assisting in his country's governance. With this freedom, Amin was able to pursue his passion for education. He spent many years studying abroad in foreign countries, including the United States, in the mid-1940s.

Amin Farid never married or had children, devoting his life to improving the education system in Arabia. He passed away peacefully in his sleep two years ago on the 3rd of June. Wait… two years ago? Opening the calendar on my laptop, I found the date of Elenore's funeral. June 3rd, 2021. Two years ago.

Clutching the letter tightly to my chest, I hoped these distant hearts finally found each other.

Subconscious Convictions

They say in the moment of tragedy, time slows down. During those precious seconds, the mind accelerates. Your surroundings blur and disappear as your attention turns inward. Upon reflection, you consider the events that led you to this point and what you could – or should – have done differently. You think of who this will affect. You're suddenly acutely aware of every regret you have. Things you wish you had done, or words you wish you had said to people you may never see again.

What they don't tell you is that during this time of reflection, those thoughts don't matter. The steps that led you to this point have already been taken. You cannot change the past; now, you must deal with whatever comes as a consequence of your actions.

But what if those thoughts *did* matter?

~*~

I'm going to lose my job.

That was the first thought that raced through my mind as I watched the man pull a gun from beneath his baggy jacket, the same man I had passed through security only minutes before.

This was my first day on the job, and I was already going to lose it.

I spent years in college scrounging for food and borrowing my friend's couches and the back seats of their cars to have a place to sleep. I borrowed money from friends, family, and disreputable sources. None of that mattered anymore, as the hard-earned fruit of my labor would sour and rot on the first day.

The moment the glint of his pistol caught my attention, my hand was already reflexively reaching for my holster. In the mere moment it took to draw my gun and form the words on my tongue for the man to drop his weapon, I was presented with a choice. Do I fire at the man, whose own gun is pointed at the young woman behind the desk? Or do I wait and try to talk him down? If I hesitate, he could kill the woman before I fire. Or I could fire first, not giving him the chance to stand down. What if the gun was fake, and this was just an attempt at intimidation? Does this scenario meet the requirements for the rules of engagement?

With my decision made, I began to shout for the man to put down the gun. Before the last word had fled from my mouth, an explosive sound that will, from that moment on, forever haunt my waking moments rings out. I made the wrong judgment. The man pulled the trigger. Time continues to crawl by as the young woman's body drops to the ground, red misting the air and painting the wall behind her as she crumples out of sight behind the desk.

Seemingly to compensate for its slowed pace, time then speeds up. People scream and drop to the ground. A mother flings herself over her child. An elderly man clutches his chest and feints. I have little recollection of what follows. I'm sure police arrive and subdue the man, as I suddenly find myself sitting outside on the curb. Uniformed officers question me. I'm not sure what answers I give them. All I can do is stare at their holstered guns.

Three seconds. That was all the time it took for the man to pull his weapon and end someone's life. Those three seconds play on repeat over and over.

I lose my job due to my negligence. If I had followed proper procedure, I would have found the man's gun as he came through security. Out of a job and with a permanent black mark on my record, my degree and certifications become nothing more than useless pieces of paper. My brand-new car I financed is repossessed. I return to couch-surfing and lending to get through each day.

Loud sounds now terrify me. The bang of a car door closing has me reflexively reaching for a sidearm that isn't there, only for nausea to rise at the mere thought of a weapon. Red mist and a body crumbling to the ground. It only took three seconds for that man to pull his pistol and kill.

I can no longer make decisions for myself. I fear that whatever choice I make will be the wrong one, somehow causing another life to end. Second-guessing every move I make completely overwhelms my day-to-day actions. I cannot help but spiral within my own tortured thoughts to the point where I am too terrified even to move.

It only took three seconds.

~*~

The instant the man pulled the gun from his jacket, instinct led me to grab my son, push him to the tile floor, and cover his small body with my own. The only thought racing through my mind was his protection. Having only recently lost his father, I couldn't fathom losing Evan as well.

A spray of red. The body of a young woman falling to the floor, the thud of her body colliding with tile echoing in my head. What if that had been Evan? What if he were older and the one working behind the desk when someone decided that they would end his life? Who would have protected him if I wasn't here?

The security guard by the door, frozen with his gun raised, solidifies my resolve that no one can protect Evan as I can.

It takes three police officers to pry me from my son's protection. Only after several reassurances that the gunman has been subdued and that we are safe am I willing to detach myself from Evan. Sweeping my sobbing four-year-old into my arms, I hold him close as I provide the police with my statement, receive the okay from medical personnel to leave, and speed toward the safety of our small home.

That could have been Evan standing behind the counter. No one can protect him like I can.

With school shootings a very real possibility, I pull Evan out of school just in case. I found a new job, allowing me to work from home while homeschooling Evan simultaneously. Groceries are delivered to the house, contact-free, of course.

The only times I find myself unable to avoid leaving our home's safety are for regular visits to the doctor's office. I put these off for as long as possible without risking Evan's health. Every individual we pass is a threat, as who knows what weapons they carry hidden beneath their clothing. Who knows their intentions or when they might decide to take their frustrations out on my innocent child?

A local news broadcast covers the story of an injured criminal waking up during surgery and attacking the caretakers and two bystanders. What if Evan and I had been there for an appointment? Even the hospitals weren't safe anymore. I called and canceled Evan's upcoming check-up.

The doctor's office called at least once a day for a week straight to reschedule Evan's appointment. I let every call ring to voicemail. I know what is best for Evan. No one can protect him like I can. The phone calls eventually stopped.

The following week, two police officers arrived at our house, claiming the hospital staff called asking for them to ensure we were okay. Through the closed door, I reiterated that all was well but refused to open my home to them. I can see from the window the weapons they carry. What if they are not real police officers? What if they are here to hurt Evan?

The next day, the police returned with a woman dressed in a pantsuit claiming to be from Child Protective Services. I refuse them entry and tell Evan to hide in his room. The woman claims that she is worried for my son's well-being and begs me to open the door.

She doesn't have to worry about Evan. That is my job. Only I can protect him.

They took Evan from me! They came in force, showing me documents that meant nothing to me as I sat handcuffed on my couch. They claim I am not mentally fit to take care of my son, as if they know anything about me or the dangers the outside world presents to my innocent child. I try to get them to understand that he needs me, that only I can protect him! Why can't they understand? They tell me I can argue my case in court.

Why does no one understand? How can no one see how

dangerous the world is? It only takes one man with a gun to decide to end a life.

No one can protect Evan as I can.

~*~

The customer service smile I have plastered on my face falls away as the man across the desk from me reaches beneath his jacket and pulls free a pistol. Despite the situation, I find myself surprised by the gun's condition. My father was an avid weapon collector, and as his only child, I was subjected to hours of instruction on all topics involving firearms. The man's gun is nothing special; it's a brand that most households have stashed away for home defense.

What caught my attention was the poor condition of the weapon. Scuffs and scratches cover most of the surface, and bare metal glints through gouged paint and texture. Wherever this man had obtained the gun from, there was a good chance it was either stolen or sold illegally.

When the last remnants of my smile disappear, and my quick analysis of the man's pistol ends, I realize too late that I am the target of his aggression.

Raised by a gun enthusiast, I thought I had seen them from every angle. I realized then that never have I stared down the barrel of one. It was a sight that immediately burned into my mind and one I never wanted to see again. I watch in slow motion as the muscles just under the skin of the man's hands tense, and his finger begins to pull the trigger. I can't help but think with irony that I won't have to worry about living with that fear.

Silence follows the explosion of a firing pistol.

~*~

The scene before me is familiar, though I can't determine why or how. I stand before a young woman, a waist-high desk the only barrier between us. My right hand grips the cold, unfamiliar metal of the pistol I purchased from a stranger earlier this morning. I stare down the top of the gun at the young woman. She seems more interested in the details of the weapon rather than the fact that it is aimed directly at her.

There is something… familiar about this woman, though I am sure I have never met her before.

An irritating itch nags in the back of my mind that something here isn't right. I have been here before. But where am I? I want to turn and take in my surroundings but cannot move anything other than my eyes. Time seems to have slowed to a near pause.

Glancing at the desk's surface, I notice a stack of credit card flyers. Oh, that's right, I'm at a bank. It is one of the few left that handles cash instead of digital currency.

Why am I at the bank?

The memories come slowly, like I am recollecting them through a vat of honey. The images are hazy at first but slowly become clearer.

I am desperate. The company I worked at collapsed due to fraud. As an accounting associate, I was one of the prime suspects in the case. It has been two years since I was accused as an accomplice, and the investigation is ongoing.

In those two years, my entire life fell apart. My fiancé left me, taking the word of the media over the man she planned to marry. She took our unborn child with her, refusing to allow me any part in the child's life. Due to the investigation, I can't find a job.

I lost my fiancé, child, and career. I lost all reason to continue to try. All I have left is a roof over my head; even that will be gone unless I do something.

Robbing the bank wasn't a thought-out plan but a decision made in desperation. Why had I thought this would be a good idea? I've never done anything like this before. This isn't me. Who have I become?

The eyes of the woman before me begin to widen as she realizes she is staring down the barrel of my gun. Realization, surprise, fear, and acceptance cross her features within a few heartbeats.

My hand tenses, my index finger beginning to pull the trigger.

Wait…

I've been here before. I've done this before. I've killed this woman already. Why am I doing this? For money? Is this really how far I have fallen? Would I seriously consider killing a woman for whatever change she might have in the drawer?

Wait, no. I have already considered this. In fact… I have already done it. I am staring down the sights of my gun into the eyes of a dead woman. That is why she is familiar to me.

I know I've killed her, but I don't remember what happened afterward. Was I arrested? Was I shot?

Glancing to my right, I notice a woman in the process of throwing herself over a young boy. Her son, Evan.

Evan? Why do I know the boy's name? That isn't all I know. I know that the mother will be so scarred from my actions that she will hide her child away from the world, paranoid and plagued by the idea of some stranger hurting the only family she has left. Evan will spend the rest of his childhood in the foster care system.

I've never met them before, so why do I know this?

I shift my attention to my left, where a young security guard points his firearm in my direction, his mouth open in a silent shout. I can see the fear and indecision wrought into his features. Due to my actions today, he will lose his job and any semblance of a healthy life.

Finally, I look back to the woman before me. She loses her life because of me. These are my victims. I can see the consequences these innocent bystanders will spend the remainder of their lives trying to cope with. All because I was desperate to pay my rent.

I don't want this. I don't want to kill this young woman who has done nothing to wrong me. I don't want to cause the security guard to spend the rest of his life terrified of strangers and loud noises. I don't want Evan to grow up without his mother.

My hand relaxes, and the gun soundlessly clatters to the ground before everything fades to black.

~*~

Looking up from the report scrolling across his tablet, Jarred smiled at his supervisor, Doctor Daniells, who had just entered the lab.

"Good afternoon, Doctor. The subject passed on the first run. His remorse caused a shift in his subconscious, and he dropped the gun before killing the woman this time."

Doctor Daniells nodded, a bit of the ever-present tension in his shoulders relaxing. "That is good. Pull him out of the simulator and send the report to the recovery team. With luck, he'll be eligible for reintegration within the next year or so."

After receiving the affirmative from his associate, Doctor Daniells headed for the door, sparing one last glance at the man lying on the bed connected to the simulator unit.

The device was revolutionary in solving overcrowding within the municipal system. Based on their progress with therapists and reports provided by behavioral specialists, qualified convicts are removed from their cells and transferred to one of a few facilities housing advanced neurological simulators. Rather than spend years within a cell of bars and mortar, they are imprisoned within the walls of their own subconscious. They are then subjected to relive the events of the crime they committed, as well as experience first-hand the impact their misconduct left on their victims.

The results were astounding, proving that remorse and guilt, if stressed on a deeply subconscious level, could change an individual's morality. Rather than spend the remainder of their lives behind bars, these ex-convicts would receive a second chance. Depending on their results after undergoing intense therapy, they would be allowed to reintegrate into a controlled section of society, a sector that was developed specifically for these individuals. They would not be allowed to return to the public, as retribution is still demanded for their actions. They would, however, be provided the opportunity to work in their chosen profession, earn a wage, and make something better of themselves while serving out the remainder of their sentence.

Tearing his gaze from the man lying in the hospital bed, Doctor Daniells stepped out of the room and headed for the next lab.

Verdant Touch

Wild and flourishing, the ivy grew, rushing along the surface of the stone wall. The creeping foliage found every imperfection, nook, crack, and cranny with which to use as a purchase. Reaching the top and spilling over and out of sight, the growth slowed to a stop. With a small smile, Elara removed her hand from once was an old, rusted torch mount.

Gasps from behind startled her, and she turned to see a small group of women standing a few yards away. Forcing a practiced smile, Elara bowed and moved quickly along the road. She had no clear destination in mind, only the desire to escape from her sudden audience. Glancing down at her hands, small and unblemished, she donned the thick cotton gloves she never went without.

Ever since the night of Elara's sixth birthday, she could turn almost anything she touched into plant life. Despite her best attempts to tame the ability, she lacked any control over what species of flora her ability created nor the extent to which it grew. The people in her small town of Woodshire considered her ability a gift from the gods. Elara, however, saw her "gift" as a curse rather than a blessing. No one knew what brought on this sudden ability, as she had a relatively simple and uneventful upbringing until the morning she awoke to find her small room transformed into a thicket of trees, flowers, and ivy.

Initially terrified of the townspeople's reactions, her parents tried to keep her ability hidden. Under the cover of night, they had traveled to the temples in the city capital, looking for a healer or bishop to heal her. Rather than perform any such healing, she was told that her gifts were just that, and she would be wise to embrace such a touch from the heavens rather than hide and risk offending the gods.

Elara was sent to live within the walls of Woodshire's church. To ensure the general populace's acceptance of her new gifts, the head bishop announced her abilities to the public as a blessing upon their small town.

"This is a sign that our prayers are not going unheard! The blessing bestowed upon this young girl proves that our efforts of reverence have not gone unnoticed. Bow your heads, my good people, and thank the gods for their blessing!"

While Elara received praise and was treated with reverence, the townspeople kept their distance. Even though her ability brought forth the beauty of nature, an innate fear was rooted in every person who neared her that a single touch would cause them to become one of her transformations. Too terrified to test this theory, Elara spent the next twenty years of her life never knowing the touch of another living being, human or animal.

As far as Elara knew, only natural flora was safe from her touch. She often spent most of her free time in the woods outside the towns' walls rather than inside. She felt like a nuisance even within the church, where one would think she was comfortable. Every person she passed bowed their heads respectfully while giving a wide berth to avoid her. Most seemed too afraid to speak with her, as though inviting conversation was enough to trigger her gift.

Having no effect on plant-made items, such as clothing, she kept her hands covered in thick cotton gloves, which was enough to keep her ability at bay. Even that security did nothing to convince the locals that it was safe to interact with her. The few who tried were uncomfortable, eager to keep their distance or escape altogether.

Elara returned to the church as the sun moved to dip below the ridge of the mountains in the west. Evening mass had already ended, and she was relieved to find the halls of the large stone structure empty. Just as she reached the door to her room, the sound of someone clearing their throat caught her attention. Turning, she found one of the newest nuns standing twenty feet away. The young woman bowed quickly.

"The bishop would like a word with you before you retire for the evening." Her eyes nervously fluttered between Elara and the woman's clasped hands. Her knuckles were nearly white with the force of her grip. Elara donned her usual pleasant smile, which had become more of a mask than genuine emotion.

"Thank you, Sister Annette. I will head to his chambers now."

The young woman bowed quickly before turning and fleeing down the hall. With one last longing glance at the door to her room, Elara headed back the way she had come, taking a branching hallway that led to the bishop's chambers. Ensuring her gloves were in place, she knocked and waited for permission before entering. The ancient man was bent over his large desk, one of the few pieces of furniture in his chambers. She waited until he raised his head before bowing respectfully.

"Ah, Elara, thank you for coming so quickly." Raising shakily from his chair, he moved to stand beside his desk but came no closer. Usually, he would invite his visitors to sit. She had never received such an invitation and did not expect one now. Clearing his throat, the older man motioned to a sheet of parchment on his desk.

"We have received a missive from Daralon, the capital city." Elara's interest piqued, but she remained silent. "Well, *you* have received a missive." Along with the disbelief that anyone would have reason to contact her specifically, she found herself bothered that rather than deliver a message that had been for her, the man had taken it upon himself to read it first.

"And what is the purpose of this missive, Your Grace?"

"It is a summons. King Alden has requested an audience. He is sending an entourage to fetch you and return to the kingdom within a fortnight."

Elara was struck silent, unsure how to respond or even what to think. Though revered as some gift from the heavens, she had been ultimately ignored for most of her life. To think that her existence was even known to the King was difficult to fathom, much less that he requested an audience with her. To state that he "requested" an audience wasn't quite right, as she surely had no right to refuse. The bishop seemed to know this if his bothered expression was anything to go by. Sighing, he returned to his chair and sat down heavily.

"I am sure you understand the importance of this request. I cannot imagine why the King would summon you, but we cannot ignore his command." Despite how correct he may be, Elara tried not to be offended at the insinuation that she was not important enough to be of any interest. "You will spend from tomorrow until the retinue arrives preparing for court. I have asked Sister Katarina to train you in proper etiquette to ensure you do not embarrass yourself and, in turn, our church. You are to report to Sister Katarina first thing in the morning. You may go."

After a respectful bow, Elara headed back to her chambers. She did not remember returning to her rooms, preparing for bed, or crawling under the sheets. Deep into the night, she still lay awake, questions racing through her mind. Replaying any significant events in the last twenty-six years of her life, she could not think of a single instance important enough to warrant an audience with the King, especially one such as King Alden. The man was known for being abrasive and unforgiving in his rule. Though he avoided causing undue wars during his reign, which could not be said for many of his predecessors, he was steadfast in his rule and allowed little room for argument.

By the time Elara had finally begun to drift to sleep, the first tinges of dawn crept through her small window. Groaning, she forced herself from her warm sheets. She mentally and physically prepared for the unforgiving tutelage that the church's oldest and most devout woman, Sister Katarina, was known for.

Until the morning that the King's entourage arrived, Elara spent every day from dawn until dusk learning the rules of court. How to speak, or rather how to not speak unless spoken to. How to avoid the gaze of anyone in higher standing than herself, which was practically everyone. She was even taught how to eat appropriately if invited to dine. Elara would have never thought there were so many rules to something as simple as eating! The only lessons she truly enjoyed were how to dance, though she doubted anyone would be willing to twirl on the dance floor with a woman known for creating foliage with a simple touch. Her dancing partner during her lessons was an overstuffed flour sack with protruding broom handles for arms.

With hardly any fanfare, twenty armored men on horseback and a single carriage arrived early one morning. The only person who came to see Elara off was the bishop, who sternly reminded her that any impressions she left during the trip would ultimately reflect upon not only the town but the church as well. Her nerves and emotions were too much of a mess to feel the offense that she should have.

Placing her few belongings in a small compartment in the rear of the carriage, her journey out of the town and onto the only road leaving the settlement had just as much fanfare as the escort's arrival had. Elara didn't even bother to push back the carriage's curtained windows to see if any of the townspeople, including her parents, had gathered to watch the procession.

The first day of travel was blissfully uneventful. Elara had yet to speak to a single soul in her escort. The only information she had gathered from her observations was that the man leading the procession was a Captain named Kael, which she had overheard when he introduced himself to the bishop. Though she had heard his name through the gap in his large helm, he had not removed the armor, and she had no idea what he looked like. Nor did she know what any of her escorts looked like, as they had all been similarly garbed in thick, shining armor, adorned only by the kingdom's crest of crossed arrows on their chests. The only feature distinguishing the captain from the rest of the ensemble was a large, deep blue cloak hanging from his left shoulder.

When they finally stopped for the first night on the road, Elara was unsure what to do with herself. Part of her wanted to hide in her carriage, even if that meant she would forgo dinner. Another voice within her argued that since these were soldiers and not simple townsfolk, she might be able to engage them in conversation without fear of them shying from her presence. The decision was made for her when a knock sounded at the small door. Before she could respond, the door opened, and she spied the captain just beyond, his cloak billowing slightly in the evening breeze.

"We have set up your accommodations, My Lady. You are welcome to retire to something more comfortable unless you'd rather stay in here."

Elara shook her head, and the captain stepped back, giving her room to emerge from the cramped carriage. The first thing she noticed as she tried to stretch her aching back subtly was that they had stopped at a large clearing alongside the road. Several campfires had already been constructed with bedrolls spread nearby. Armored soldiers milled about preparing cookfires and performing other miscellaneous chores. Next to the carriage was the only tent, obviously intended for her use.

Elara felt immediately embarrassed at the treatment. It felt awkward that she was the only one sleeping in a tent while the rest were exposed to the elements. That thought, however, was not what made her uneasy the most. The soldiers were still fully donned in their armor, including their helmets.

"Do your men sleep in their armor?" She found herself asking before she could think better of it.

Shocked, the captain looked back at her. She hadn't noticed

that he had moved to hold open the tent flap for her. His gaze swept over the soldiers before returning to her.

"It is a sign of respect, My Lady. They will stay covered while in your presence."

This was going to be a long week of travel if this was standard practice.

"Please, do not let my presence make you or your men uncomfortable. I hardly see why my being here would require you to remain armored. I understand the need while traveling, but at camp, surely you allow your soldiers to relax after a hard day's ride?"

She didn't mean to sound accusatory, realizing only after the fact that she might have come across as so. After an awkward silence, Elara noticed that the soldiers around them had stopped and were all looking at their captain. She wished she could see their expressions so that she could have some indication of how badly she had just messed up.

With a loud snort of laughter, which startled her, the captain dropped the tent flap and removed his helm, revealing clean-cut sandy brown hair, a strong jaw covered in stubble, and warm brown eyes.

With a lopsided smile, he bowed his head slightly to her before turning to his men. "You all heard the Lady. No reason to be so formal."

A chorus of cheers released from the group as the men began pulling their helms and armor off. Elara hadn't realized how uncomfortable her escorts had been until they sent grateful smiles and nods in her direction. Their simple milling about turned into motivated preparation of meals. Elara felt the tension in her shoulders slowly start to ebb away.

The captain turned back to her again, bowing at the waist.

"I feel I must apologize. My intent was not to make you uncomfortable but to give you a sense of security. We were told you have never been to Daralon before and were worried you might feel a little out of your element. I am Kael, and I am at your service."

Kael rose and gave her another lopsided smile, which she found strangely endearing. The genuine friendliness she felt from him allowed for the last of her tension to melt away.

"Please, don't apologize. You're correct that I feel a little apprehensive about leaving my home. But I would rather you and your soldiers be comfortable. Otherwise, this will be a long trip."

He nodded and gestured toward the tent. "You are welcome to retire if you'd like. I will have one of my men bring you food shortly. I'm afraid it may not be as nice as you're used to, as food preparation can be a little restrictive when traveling."

Elara looked toward the tent, then back at the campfires, which seemed much more inviting. She allowed the request to sit near a fire to go unspoken, knowing such an action would only make the captain and whoever she sat near uncomfortable.

Kael seemed to notice her hesitation, answering her unspoken request. "If you're not yet ready to retire, you are always welcome to join us."

Surprised by his invitation, Elara shook her head and slipped on her mask of a practiced smile, pleasant yet showing no real emotion. "That is quite alright. I do not want to impose or make anyone uncomfortable with my presence."

Kael's lopsided smile dropped, and he tipped his head slightly to the side. Elara was reminded of a curious dog. "Why would your presence make anyone uncomfortable?"

"Well, because..." Her words trailed off. She thought it would have been obvious. Did he not know of her ability? Or of the threat that her touch possessed? Unsure what to say, she instead gestured to her gloved hands. The confusion lifted from the captain's features, his smile returning and amusement gleaming in his eyes.

"Since we are in the middle of the forest, I don't see any issue with you creating a few more trees or bushes. Although I would request that you refrain from changing any of our camping supplies, as those are quite difficult to replace out here."

Elara, once again, found herself speechless. So he *was* aware of her ability, though he showed no apprehension toward it. She noticed then how closely they were standing, much closer than most would dare. The urge to step away itched at her, and she shuffled in place to placate the sensation.

"Are you not afraid I might turn one of your men into... well, anything?"

He brought one of his armored hands to his chin and contemplated her question. He gazed over her, pausing momentarily at her gloved hands before continuing his examination. Elara felt exposed, resisting the need to cover herself. Her cheeks warmed under his scrutiny. His inspection finished, he asked, "Have you ever done that before? Turned someone into vegetation?"

"Well, no. Not exactly."

He nodded as if satisfied with her answer. "Then what should I be worried about? As I understand it, we should be safe as long as you have those gloves on. Is that right?"

Elara glanced at her gloves, then back at the man before her. How could he take this so lightly? "That is the idea, yes."

"Well then," Kael gestured with his arm to the field of campfires. "Please feel free to mingle. These are my best soldiers, and I hope you will find them pleasant company."

He left her then to join his men. Unsure what to do, Elara turned to study the gathering. With most of their armor removed, she was stunned to see that this troop was not just men but men *and* women. Women were not allowed to take up arms in her town, whether to join the town guard or hunt in the surrounding woods.

With one last glance at her tent, she approached the fires and the enthusiastic soldiers surrounding them.

Despite long hours in the carriage, the procession's travel through the forested country went by quickly. Each morning and evening, Elara shared her meal with a different group of soldiers. Though she was asked many questions about her abilities, no one showed any alarm or fear. Each group she joined for the evening welcomed her openly. After the first two nights, Kael began joining her around the cookfires. She had expected the soldiers to stiffen and act respectfully when their captain joined their midst. However, their merriment increased, each man and woman cheering and raising a tankard or flask when Kael sat beside her.

The nightly revelry was initially overwhelming for Elara. Fearing her presence would make the townspeople uncomfortable, she watched from afar as they celebrated weddings and festivals. She felt horribly out of place to be among the singing and conversations but feared her early departure would be seen as offensive. Just as she floundered for an excuse to retire for the evening, Kael would save her by requesting her to join him for a quiet walk before turning in for the night. These moments quickly became something she looked forward to.

While they picked their way around the outskirts of the campsites, close enough not to lose sight of the soldiers but far enough for a semblance of privacy, the two spent nearly an hour each night sharing stories of their past. Kael recounted his experience of rising through the ranks of the King's Royal Army, sharing stories of far-off battles and skirmishes that nearly cost him his life. He spoke of men and women he had lost, his voice hardly more than a whisper at times until trailing off entirely. Elara allowed the silence to envelop them, unsure how to console him for his loss and desperate to lend a comforting hand. The urge terrified her, as she found herself on multiple occasions reaching toward him.

For the first time since childhood, she confided in Kael about her deepest desire to be free of her gift and how she felt she was cursed rather than blessed. He hadn't reprimanded her as she had expected and feared.

"I cannot imagine how it must feel," he said, "to fear the touch of another. It is such a simple act that I never realized I took for granted before. I'm so-"

"Please don't apologize," she quickly cut him off. "It took a while to get used to avoiding those around me, but I have had over two decades to get used to it. It was hard at first, admittedly. Especially when I couldn't hug my own parents in farewell when they turned me over to the church."

"Elara…" Kael's voice was soft, not with pity, but sympathy. A knot she hadn't noticed was forming in her chest, and it loosened as she met his gaze, every bit as soft as his voice. She hadn't realized they had stopped walking.

Suddenly feeling immensely awkward under his intense gaze, she cleared her throat and waved a hand dismissively. "As I said, I have become used to it. Anyway," She stepped around him, resuming their walk. "Do you know why the King has summoned me? I've just about driven myself insane trying to figure it out."

"Unfortunately, I do not. King Alden can be a little overbearing but is a worthy ruler. Whatever his reason is, it isn't something you should fear."

Much to Elara's disappointment, it seemed no one knew why she had been summoned by the King, leaving her to spend her hours on the road in speculation.

On the twelfth day of the journey, they emerged from the woods onto a large, open plain. The sudden lack of trees was shocking to Elara. Not only because she had spent her entire life enveloped by the dense wood but also because the change was so drastic that it hardly seemed natural. Peering from her window, she saw why. Stumps littered the ground on either side of the road where trees had been severed. The skeletal remains of bushes and shriveled patches of grass filled the landscape between the stumps.

Even in her Woodshire, they toppled trees for coal, firewood, and structures. But never before had she seen deforestation on such a large scale. When the escort stopped for the evening, there was a visible shift in the soldiers' demeanor. Though still good-natured, they were more quiet and reserved than before. Rather than boisterous singing and laughing, as she had grown used to, the men and women kept to their small groups and either spoke silently amongst themselves or kept silent. Elara wondered at the change but was afraid to ask. Though subdued, the company was still agreeable.

The remaining days of travel showed much of the same scenery. Lifeless plains as far as Elara could see, with evidence of deforestation. Finally, on the fifteenth day since leaving

Woodshire, the walls and spires of the capital city could be seen on the horizon.

Elara hadn't realized how comfortable she had become with her escort over the past two weeks until the realization dawned on her that her travels were at an end. Upon finally setting her sights on the looming city and hearing that they would reach the gates just before nightfall, Elara's nerves and fears roared back.

As the open gates neared and Elara could see crowds gathering, she closed the curtains. Any comfort she had felt with the men and women of her escort was quickly forgotten. Murmurs of the crowd filled her small carriage, and Elara had to stop herself from shrinking in her seat as though curious eyes could see her through the drawn curtains.

Fearful scenarios played out in her mind. She knew the King had only summoned her because of her gift, but there was no telling if that was good. Perhaps the man hated the natural world if the massive deforestation was anything to go by. Maybe he found her gift unnatural and planned to have her executed. What if she accidentally touched something while in audience with the King and destroyed the throne room? Or worse, what if someone accidentally touched her?

The sudden stop of the carriage brought Elara out of her thoughts. Kael opened the door moments later and stepped back so that she could climb out. It was weird to see him fully donned in his armor, his helm hiding his expression. She longed to see his lopsided smile, reassuring her that everything would be okay.

As she stepped from the carriage, Elara took in her surroundings. The group had stopped at the base of a large staircase. The sheer size and width of the stairs seemed quite excessive to her, wide enough to fit ten men walking abreast with room to spare. At the distant top of the stairs, the castle loomed. Elara had to crane her head back to see its distant spires, which nearly touched the clouds. All around her was stone. The road was paved, and every building within sight was made of the same material formed into bricks. Every surface seemed to blend into each other. Despite her awe at the size of the castle, Elara found it disturbingly unnatural. There were no lawns, bushes, trees, or flora of any kind.

Noticing that Kael had begun the long trek up the stairs, Elara rushed to walk alongside him. While she had been distracted by her surroundings, he had dismissed his soldiers. Her lungs burned as they finally reached the top. She struggled to hide her exertion, impressed with how unaffected Kael seemed after the climb, especially considering how much extra weight his armor undoubtedly added.

A small entourage of men and women garbed in finely tailored outfits of blue and silver greeted them at the top. Introductions were made, though any words exchanged were instantly forgotten as they moved through two massive wooden doors. Upon direction, Elara followed the retinue, Kael close behind.

Several massive and expensively furnished corridors later, she finally stood in a mighty throne room. Though Elara had never seen a throne room before, she assumed that was where she stood, as the only piece of furniture in the massive domed room was an oversized ornately upholstered chair upon a tall dais. Torches lined the room's walls, though only a few were lit, casting deep shadows. The darkness frightened Elara, and she wondered why they didn't light the rest of the torches. If it was a tactic to frighten her, it had worked.

Seated upon the magnificent chair atop the dais was King Alden himself. Having only heard stories of the man, Elara was not sure what to expect. The man was imposing, even so far away. Even from afar, she could tell he was far taller than her. His ornate blue and silver clothing was of the finest quality, the silver fabric gleaming in the faint torchlight. Long black hair was pulled back into a tight bun, and a thick, cleanly trimmed beard shaped his face. Overwhelmed by the room and the King's appearance, Elara didn't initially notice the King glaring down at her.

Elara's heart rate increased under the weight of the King's glower. As the silence dragged on, she had to resist the urge to fidget or shuffle in place. Was she supposed to speak first? Captain Kael had moved upon entering to stand to the left of the dais. She glanced at him for help but couldn't see his expression under his helm. He bowed his head at her ever so slightly, flicking his hand toward the king.

Sudden horror filled Elara. Scrambling, she curtsied before the King. This was the first lesson Sister Katarina had drilled into her, and she had already forgotten. Her face burned as she held her curtsy.

"Rise."

The single word echoed through the massive room. Elara wondered if that was why the room had been structured the way it was. Legs trembling, she stood and raised her gaze to the King, careful to keep from meeting his. She picked a spot over his shoulder and fixed her gaze on it.

"Elara Farrington from Woodshire. Do you know why I have summoned you here?"

It took two attempts for Elara to respond. "No, Your Majesty." Her voice broke on the title, and she winced.

"It has come to my attention that you possess the touch of nature. Is this true?"

"Yes, Your Majesty."

"Show me."

Sheer panic rose within Elara. Though she had intentionally released her abilities before, it had always been outside, near the woods, and with no one around. She was now enclosed within multiple stone walls, with no nature in sight, and before an audience. She glanced nervously around before looking again at the King.

"Right... right now, Your Majesty?"

The glare directed at her intensified. "Yes, now. Is that a problem?"

"I..." She swallowed and glanced around again. "I need something manufactured to use as a resource, Your Majesty. I cannot create something from nothing."

Without prompting, Kael removed his helm. He stepped away from the dais and placed the helmet in her gloved hands. She must have looked as terrified as she felt, for he smiled encouragingly at her before stepping back to his place.

Hands shaking, she held the helmet. She had never been able to control her ability as far as deciding what would grow or how substantial the growth would be. The nature that burst from her touch seemed to have a mind of its own. She considered insisting that they step outside, but her voice stuck in her throat. What if nothing happened at all? What if, for the first time since her ability first appeared, her touch caused no reaction at all? Such a thing was a dream she had long since given up on, but for some reason, it was a very real fear at the moment.

Lost in her fears, she was startled when Kael cleared his

throat, the sound echoing in the empty chamber. Her eyes snapped from the helm back to him. She met his gaze, and he nodded at her. Taking a deep breath, she lifted one hand and used her teeth to pinch the fabric of the middle finger and remove her glove. Glancing again at Kael and then the king, she rested her hand on the still-warm metal.

Brown and green burst forth from the steel, shooting toward the ceiling. Gasping, Elara dropped the helm. If it clattered when hitting the tile floor, the sound was drowned out by creaking and rustling. Too terrified to see what had happened, Elara slammed her eyes shut and covered them with her hands for good measure. Eventually, the sounds quieted, the large room descending into silence.

Slowly, Elara opened her eyes, peering between her fingers. Several feet before her stood a massive oak, its branches reaching far above toward the ceiling and out wide to scrape against the windows and stone walls. Despite its large size, the only damage Elara could see was from the massive roots, which had cracked the floor tile to bury deep in the ground.

The tree blocked her view of the King, and she considered hiding behind the trunk. Curiosity overrode her fear, and she stepped around the massive base to see King Alden on his feet, staring at the oak in awe and astonishment. Glancing around the room, she noticed that everyone, Kael included, shared the same expression.

A smile crept across the King's features, which Elara found more disturbing than his glare. With his gaze still locked on the tree, he descended the stairs of the dais. Elara moved to stand beside Kael as the man paced fully around the oak until he returned to stand before Elara. She tensed, awaiting his verdict. Was he offended? Would he order her execution?

"Elara Farrington. I have summoned you here today because you are the only one who can save this kingdom."

Tears that had already begun to well in fear clouded her vision as she blinked in confusion. She glanced at Kael at her side, but his astonished gaze was still focused on the oak in the center of the throne room.

"Save the kingdom, Your Majesty?"

"Yes." The King finally pulled his attention from the massive tree and faced her fully, his hands clasped behind his back. He was a full head and a half taller than her, though she felt even smaller under his intense gaze. "I am sure you noticed this on your travels, but there are no trees or growth for miles surrounding Daralon. I fear the quick advancement of my city's development has destroyed the soil. My people cannot survive for much longer with so few resources. Farmlands are infertile. Trees will no longer grow, meaning we have no wood or coal without having it imported. Herds and game have ventured so far that our hunters have returned empty-handed for weeks. Even livestock hardly survive. I fear for the future of my people."

To Elara's utter astonishment, the King looked away, guilt reflected clearly in his dark eyes. He seemed lost in thought, and Elara waited for him to continue. Finally, the King sighed and looked again at the massive oak. "However, you and you alone can save this kingdom and my people with your gift."

"I am not sure that I can, Your Majesty." At her admission, every set of eyes snapped to her. Kael looked panicked while the King's glower returned.

"You would refuse your king?"

"No! No, Your Majesty. It is just that... I have no control over this gift. I may be able to summon nature at a simple

94

touch, but I have no say in what grows or to what extent. I am afraid that I might cause more harm than good."

She stared at her feet, too ashamed to look at the man before her. Even though she did not know why she had been brought here until now, she felt she had failed. She saw Kael reach for her out of the corner of her eye. She stepped away from him and returned her glove to her exposed hand. His arm dropped back to his side.

Saying nothing, the King resumed his pacing around the oak. After two passes, he stopped again before Elara.

"Look at me."

She flinched against the harshness of his tone before lifting her gaze to meet his. His glower was gone despite his tone, replaced with a softness she did not think he could possess.

"Will you not try? My people are starving. Surely, you noticed how few torches are lit in my halls. We do not have the resources to continue as we have. In desperation, nearly all wood in my city has been replaced by stone. I do not deny that the scar on this land is anyone's fault but mine and my forefathers. I will not allow this mistake to be repeated. Hundreds, if not thousands, of innocent people will either die or be forced to leave their homes if I do not find a solution. I have tried all I can, and you are my last hope. Do not do this because your king demands it; do it because people will suffer if you don't. Please."

Stunned, Elara could not find her voice. How could anyone deny him after so heartfelt a claim? She nodded her consent.

By the following midday, Elara was surrounded by miles of empty landscape in every direction. Despite the lavish room she had been given last night, Elara could not sleep, plagued by all the possibilities of what could go wrong should she release her abilities on such a large scale. Still terrified and now sleep-deprived, she felt on the verge of hysteria.

Accompanying her was a small contingent of ten soldiers, including Kael. Despite the support he had shown her throughout their brief time together, she could not bring herself to look to him for encouragement this time. She feared for the safety of the group gathered. Since stepping from her carriage, the same she had traveled in before, she had begged them to leave her for their own safety, which they promptly refused.

Along with her group of soldiers, they had brought a sizable wagon of old armor and other miscellaneous discarded items for her to use as a resource. After all, she could not make something from nothing.

Shakily accepting a rusted and dented chest piece from one of the soldiers, she stepped a few paces away from the others. Placing the piece of armor on the ground, she hesitated before removing her gloves. With one last deep breath, she rested both hands on the metal.

Greenery burst forth, this time out instead of up. Green grass flew out over the landscape as rushing water might when released from a dam. Every few feet, trees of varying species sprouted from the trunks of their ancestors. Bushes and wildflowers sprang from the ground, and Elara quickly found herself in the center of a large grove. Cheers came from behind her, muffled by the sudden vegetation. Elated, Elara released a cheer of her own.

Over the next several hours, she and her crew covered miles of empty terrain. Despite how much ground they covered, the ravaged landscape still spread for leagues in every direction. This would be no small task and would take weeks, if not months, to repair the damage to the land. Despite the overwhelming task, Elara felt that, for once in her life, she had a purpose.

That evening, a grand celebration was held throughout the city. Though the feast was kept meager due to their already low food supply, the revelry did not diminish. The city folk, with open arms and plentiful praises, welcomed Elara. She froze in terror the first time someone patted her on the back. Although her ability was only released through her hands, she was still unaccustomed to the touch of another person.

Several hours and a few drinks later, Elara sat on the ledge of a large fountain in one of the many town squares. She had lost count of how many people she had met, songs she had danced to, and stories she had heard. She was often asked to replicate her gift, some even handing her something of their belonging to use as a resource. She was thankfully saved by Kael each time, who stated she needed to save her energy for the weeks ahead. Elara wasn't sure if there was a limit to her ability but was grateful nonetheless.

With some time to herself, partygoers still celebrating in groups around her, Elara removed her gloves, staring at her hands. Smooth and unblemished. Since she was a child, she had hated her hands. Her gift was destructive, destroying anything man-made and instilling fear in those around her. She felt proud of her ability for the first time in her life.

"Didn't have too much to drink, did you?"

Elara startled. Caught off balance on the fountain's ledge, she fell back towards the water. Just before she would have hit the surface, a hand grabbed her own, pulling her forward. She came face to face with a laughing Kael. He was finally not in a suit of armor, instead blending in with the civilians around him with a simple pair of breeches and a clean tunic.

"Careful. It may be summer, but the nights are cold and perhaps not the best time for a swim."

Elara hadn't heard what he said and didn't respond as she stared in horror. He still held her hand. Her ungloved hand. Tears sprang unbidden to her eyes as she screwed them shut. She had felt fear before but never terror such as this. She couldn't bring herself to open her eyes to see what had become of Kael. He had been the first to treat her like a normal person, not as some "blessed" being to be feared and hidden from view. And now that same ability she had finally learned to accept had surely killed the man.

"Elara? Are you alright?"

At the sound of his voice, her eyes sprung open. Kael stood before her, his hand still holding hers, concern etched his features.

"You're alive…" Her voice came out in hardly more than a whisper.

Kael's features bunched up in confusion. He looked down at himself, then back at her. "Yes, it would certainly seem so. Should I not be?"

"You…" She swallowed. "You're touching me."

Kael glanced at their joined hands. After a moment, confusion gave to surprise, then joy.

"So I am."

Slowly, he reached with the hand that wasn't holding hers for her other free, ungloved one. She flinched away but was not quick enough. Threading their fingers together, they both stared in amazement.

No greenery appeared; neither ivy nor trees sprouted from his skin.

Tears streaming down her face, Elara broke out in laughter. For the last twenty years of her life, she feared the touch of another, unsure what would happen should her ability be triggered. As it turned out, nothing would have happened at all.

Her laugh was cut short as she was suddenly pulled into an embrace by a jubilant Kael. He lifted her from the ground and spun her before setting her down again. Dropping his forehead to hers, they said nothing as the last of her tears and their shared laughs died away.

"Thank you." He whispered, his eyes closed and lopsided smile wide. Her brows furrowed.

"What are you thanking me for?"

"You've saved this kingdom. You've saved my people."

"No." Elara sighed deeply, a weight she hadn't realized had been on her shoulders since childhood finally lifting. "This kingdom saved me."

Man-Made Morals

lue eyes. Fair skin. Freckled nose. Long, healthy brown locks. Each feature of the woman standing before him seemed normal, even pretty. Yet, as he stepped back and observed, a sense of unease crept over him. There was something... off. He couldn't quite put his finger on it, and the longer he stared, the more uncanny the woman appeared. What truly sent shivers down his spine was the unnatural stillness she possessed. Clad in a simple black dress with a white apron, not even her chest moved as one would if drawing breath.

Theodore leaned towards the woman again, his mind grappling with the possibility that she wasn't real. He had tried to get her attention, waving in front of her unblinking eyes, even lightly shaking her shoulder, but she remained unresponsive as if she were a mere figment of his imagination.

Was she one of those statues made of wax he had read about? The concept was popular in museums to replicate people and animals in past ages, but why would the foyer of a wealthy Bionics Enterprise investor have one just inside the door to his home?

Even odder than the woman standing before him was the fact that he now stood within the receiving hall of his childhood and adolescent icon. Having just returned from his study abroad in England, Theodore was in a constant state of disbelief since receiving the invitation. How could he, a recent graduate with no fame, have an invitation waiting for him from the one and only Xavier Fitzgerald?

The man was notorious worldwide for his controversial work in the bionics industry. At the time, he received constant negative criticism for his experiments, which involved testing and combining bionics with the human nervous system. Xavier's dream was to create prosthetics that not only returned bodily function to amputees and paraplegics but created extremities that performed better than a natural limb ever could. Most of society frowned upon his experiments, often blaming him for trying to "play God" by altering human anatomy from natural to artificial. Yet, despite the backlash, he pushed through and accomplished precisely what he set out to do.

Against all odds, he defied the world's expectations. Instead of creating his own business, Xavier became a freelance consultant for other companies, guiding them in his innovative footsteps. Thirty years later, he still invests in these companies, profiting from the success of the industry he created, all without lifting a finger, bionic or otherwise. It was a twist no one saw coming.

Having recently completed his degree in Biomedical Engineering with a minor in Electrical Engineering and Robotics, Theodore considered Xavier his idol. Imagine the boy's surprise when the legend himself contacted his family home with the request to meet him personally.

Though passionate about his studies and receiving near-perfect marks in all subjects, Theodore couldn't understand why someone as talented as Xavier would be interested in a young student with no real-world experience. The odd woman now before him was solidifying his inclination that this was, in fact, all a dream.

If this woman was indeed fake, which he was beginning to believe was the only logical explanation, the detail the creator put into the replica was astounding. Upon close inspection, he could spy individual pores in her face, though she was blemish-free. Leaning closer, Theodore thought he could even see delicate hair follicles.

Pale blue eyes snapped to lock with his. Yelping and drop-ping the briefcase he had been holding, Theodore stumbled back from the woman, whose eyes now tracked his movements. Heart racing, Theodore righted himself and retrieved his briefcase from the ground, all without breaking eye contact with the woman. Though her eyes stayed locked to his, no other part of her moved. Goosebumps broke across his skin with the utter wrongness of the situation.

"Theodore, my boy!"

The booming voice of his idol caused the poor boy to nearly drop his briefcase again. Xavier stood at the top of a grand stairwell, his hands casually tucked in the pockets of his immaculate three-piece suit. Theodore glanced back at the woman, whose eyes were again staring unblinkingly straightforward. Shivering involuntarily, he fought the urge to recoil.

"Beautiful, isn't she?"

The clattering of his briefcase impacting the floor echoed through the chamber. Xavier stood directly behind him in-stead of at the top of the stairs, where he had been only a second before. How the man had moved so quickly and without a single sound was beyond Theodore. By all accounts, he should have heard the echo of his footsteps as he approached. His cheeks burning, Theodore moved to retrieve his briefcase from the floor.

Stepping away from the strange woman, Theodore pushed his shoulders back and stuck his hand toward his idol, praying he would survive the rest of this meeting without further embarrassment.

"Theodore Barrington, Sir. And may I say what an absolute honor it is to meet you?"

Xavier smirked, removing one of his pocketed hands to shake Theodore's. Despite being well into his sixties, the man looked remarkably young, only the beginning traces of gray peppering his thick locks of slicked-back hair.

"I'm glad you were able to come. I would have reached out sooner, but the university informed me you were completing your robotics degree overseas in England. How was that?"

"Very enlightening, Sir. They have a very different way of doing things there."

Xavier nodded and turned back toward the woman. His hands were once again tucked casually into his pockets. "Very good. Now tell me, what do you think of her? Beautiful, no?"

Theodore gnawed on the inside of his cheek, debating whether to be honest or revert to flattery.

"She is definitely… unique. Is she… um… real?"

Xavier's smirk grew into a full grin. "What do you think?"

Theodore again studied the woman, albeit reluctantly. This time, he kept his distance. She appeared just as lifeless as when he first spotted her.

"I don't think so."

Xavier turned his attention towards Theodore, brows

slightly furrowed. His grin dropped to a slight frown. "And what gives you that impression?"

Panic stabbed in the younger man's gut. Had he given the wrong answer? Did he sound too sure of himself? His mind was racing; he wasn't sure if he should point out his observations in the chance that he was wrong.

"Speculation?"

"Come now, Theo. May I call you Theo? You have to give me more than that. A well-educated man as yourself can offer more than mere speculation."

Theodore had the vague sense that he was being tested.

"Well, to begin with, she isn't breathing. She has yet to blink while I've been here, and any attempts to gain her attention have failed." He didn't mention the few seconds when the woman tracked his movements, still unsure if it had happened.

The inventor had nodded along with Theodore's explanation, his frown becoming more prominent.

"Yes, yes. That all makes sense. Such simple things, too. After spending years only looking at the big picture, you forget to remember the finer details." He said no more, seeming lost in his thoughts while staring at the woman before them. Theodore wasn't sure if he had passed the test or not. Between the woman's stare and the inventor's brooding, he put his best effort forward to avoid fidgeting.

Coming to some decision, Xavier nodded before turning and abruptly placing his hands on either of Theodore's shoulders.

"Theo, my boy, how would you like to join me and be a part of the future of robotics?"

Had it been possible, Theodore's jaw would have hit the ground. The further this day progressed, the less he believed it was real, not just a complex dream he would soon wake from.

He hoped he didn't wake up any time soon.

"M-me, Sir?"

"Yes, you."

Despite his delight at the offer, a single thought invaded Theodore's mind, wiggling to the surface. "Why me?"

At this, Xavier's brows again furrowed. "What do you mean?"

"Well…" Theodore shrugged. "I am no one, Sir. With all due respect, what would someone like me, who has no more experience than a degree, offer someone like… well, someone like *you*?"

"Your lack of experience is exactly what you can offer." Xavier chuckled at Theodore's apparent confusion. "What I am trying to do is change the future. What I have in mind differs from what anyone has seen before, and I need a young, *fresh* mind to help me. One who does not already have experience and expectations, which will ultimately hold them back from trying something new."

Leaving one hand still on his shoulder, Xavier motioned to the woman with the other.

"You were correct in your observation. She is a prototype—the result of two decades of work and the only of her kind. Five years from now, I plan to have her mass-produced. Well, not *her*, per se. But others of her kind."

Theodore again observed the woman. Rather than put at ease knowing that she wasn't real, the uncanny likeness to a real, living woman instead made him that much more uncomfortable. The fact that he could look upon her and have to observe her thoroughly to determine whether or not she was alive was disturbing to him.

"And what do you plan to do with these… beings?"

"Essentially, they are synthetic humans. Or synths, as I've

taken to calling them. Or her. As she is the only successful one so far. Just imagine…" Xavier began gesturing with his hands as he continued, his excitement palpable. "A world where you can purchase help in whatever way you need, without the worries of contract legality that comes with human services. They can be nannies, butlers, cooks, or gardeners. They can work in hazardous environments without the risk of illness or lawsuits! The possibilities are endless! A permanent helping hand without worrying about wages, insurance, or living conditions."

"So… slavery?"

"Slavery?" Xavier spat out the word as if it tasted foul. "The synths aren't real, Theodore. Just a network of wires, machinery, and electronics. Think of it as just a single bionic mass. They need no food or sustenance besides occasional maintenance, as nothing lasts forever. Just imagine the possibilities!"

As extraordinary as the concept sounded, something in the back of Theodore's mind stopped him from outright agreeing, which he found equally frustrating. The man he had spent the entirety of his childhood and many years of his adolescence idolizing was handing him his dream on a platter, a dream he hadn't even realized he had until now. To work alongside *the* Xavier Fitzgerald! He should be jumping for joy at the offer, agreeing to any proposals made by the man. However, something nagged at him, saying, 'This just doesn't seem right.'

At what point did you draw the line between what was human and what isn't? Although this woman before him looked real in every way, other than a few minor details, he knew she was fake. Yet he could not bring himself to view her as a piece of machinery, to treat her as if he were some master and she nothing more than a slave to his will.

Suppose these synths were released to the public and became an everyday staple in society. How could viewing these robots that were so lifelike not cause people to inadvertently skew their view of the people around them who really were alive? Would those unable to afford these commodities lose the labor-intensive jobs they relied on to fabricated humans?

The whole concept just seemed wrong. As strongly as he may feel about this, he couldn't bring himself to voice these concerns to his idol, lest he destroy any future chances of working alongside the man.

The man in question seemed to sense his hesitation.

"I haven't developed the technology to read minds just yet, Theo, so you'll have to tell me what you're thinking."

"Sorry, Sir. I'm just grappling with the ethical implications of what all of this entails.

"Ah yes, ethics." Xavier frowned as though he had bitten into sour fruit. "Ethical dilemmas are mere bumps on the road to progress, my boy. Consider the countless lives we could improve with our bionic creations, not to mention the economy. We have the power to change the world."

"I understand the potential benefits, Sir, but what about the essence of humanity? Are we not playing God by tampering with what it means to be human?"

Xavier swept his hands through the air as if to clear it of Theodore's reservations. "Humanity is not confined to flesh and bone. It is the capacity to innovate and transcend our limitations. Our synths will be more than mere replicas; they will be the next evolution of humanity. Embrace the future, Theodore, for it is upon us."

"But at what cost? Are we sacrificing the sanctity of life

for the sake of progress?" Theodore wondered briefly if he should stop but couldn't bring himself to now that he had begun voicing his concerns.

"Progress has never come without sacrifice, Theo. Every invention, every advancement, has faced scrutiny and resistance. No one knows that better than me." Theodore winced at his words. "But history will remember us as pioneers, visionaries who dared to defy convention and shape a better world." Xavier put both hands again on Theodore's shoulders, pleading. "Join me, Theo, and together, we shall leave a legacy that will echo through the ages."

Silence settled between them, the last of Xavier's words echoing and emphasizing his claim. Theodore longed to accept his proposal, if only for the opportunity to work alongside the man he had spent the better part of his life looking up to. His nagging conscience kept his acceptance at bay.

"Be that as it may, Sir, I… I need some time to think. This is a weighty decision, and I want to be certain I'm on the right side of history."

"Of course, my boy. Of course. Take all the time you need. But remember, the future waits for no one. It will pass you by if you don't grasp it while you can." He gave Theodore's shoulder a supportive squeeze before returning to the stairs.

Turning towards the door, Theodore stopped after two paces, the echo of his steps bouncing off marble walls and tile floor. When he stopped, so did the echoes. Turning back, he watched Xavier leisurely approach and climb the stairs. The man's footfalls left no echoing sounds as Theodore's had. As he watched, he could have sworn he saw the telltale glint of metal under the hem of both his pant legs.

Bionic legs. This explained the older man's speed and silent movements. Racking his memory, he could not remember ever hearing of any incident that would warrant the prosthetics. As closely as Theodore followed the man's research and innovations, he would know if something had happened.

Hypersensitive to his observations, Theodore noted how smoothly the older man moved. Despite his age, Xavier moved as confidently as a man younger than Theodore. After a life of study and invention, surely the man must have developed a limp, stooped back, or stiff neck. Yet the older man looked as fit as a young professional athlete.

How much of Xavier was still human?

As Theodore turned back towards the front door, movement caught his attention. It was the synth. She had turned in his direction, her eyes upon him. As he watched, frozen mid-step, her chest began moving. It lifted and fell in rhythmic succession, mimicking breathing. The small, innocent smile on her face was the last that Theodore noticed before he fled from the manor.

Fireheart

"Come on… One more time."

Bouncing on the balls of my feet, I shake out my stiff arms, hoping to shake out my anxieties as well. I stop, close my eyes, and take a deep breath, willing my mind to clear. The act takes a few seconds longer than it should, but soon, I can feel the familiar and welcome spark of energy deep within me. Magic.

Focusing all my attention on that spark, I urge it to grow. It heeds my command, warmth flooding my torso as it increases. Once satisfied with the energy built within my chest, I urge the fire to spread to my shoulders. A deep tingling spreads through my skin and muscles as the force follows my command. I next push the magic through my arms, halting at my wrists.

I allow the magic to stop there while I calm myself. This is where it keeps going wrong. One last big breath. In… and out.

I push the magic further into my hands, palms beginning to burn ever so slightly. Not nearly as much as they should, but the fact that I can feel the magic at all is a good sign. Keeping my eyes closed, I move my arms forward, spread my fingers wide, and angle my palms toward the metal target I know is several yards in front of me.

Finally, I push my magic towards my fingers and beyond,

using the direction of my palms to direct the flow of elemental flames that should burst from me. I anticipate my fingers burning with the transference of power.

Yet I feel nothing. The pent-up energy that had transferred from my core to my palms fizzles into nothing. I open my eyes and drop my arms in defeat. Such a simple spell, a beginner's spell, and I cannot do it.

My name is Soren Fireheart, and I am a Mage's Apprentice.

Since the age of twelve, I have secluded myself within the depths of the Moonshire Wood along with my master, Eamon Waterheart. Mages are few and far between, making up less than one percent of the realm's population. About ninety percent of that tiny population live in near-constant isolation, just as I do. Overall, seen as unnatural for our abilities, we are shunned from society and only called upon to use the same powers we were ostracized for to aid in a crisis.

Fifteen years ago, a forest fire broke out as the result of a few drunken kids from town who'd lost control of a small campfire. After ignoring old man Eamon's existence for years, the town called upon the mage to use his water to extinguish the fire. Once the flames were tamed, so too were the townspeople's gratitude. I was only six years old then, but I remember my fascination with the man's power. My young mind couldn't understand why he wasn't accepted in the town.

Fifteen years later, as a mage, my adult mind still cannot comprehend why our kind is not accepted into society. When I asked Eamon, he told me a story of centuries past when mages began emerging from the populace. These elemental wielders considered themselves blessed and above those without magic. Drunk on power, they used their newfound abilities to oppress the public, ruling with fear and cruelty.

In-fighting between mages was common, effectively dwindling their numbers until the common populace, tired of the authoritarian rule, came together and overthrew their self-proclaimed sovereigns.

Following the revolt, magic wielders were banished at the first signs of power, forever ostracized, and blamed for past transgressions. No one knows what causes the magic to manifest, as the trait does not pass from parent to offspring.

Years had passed since the day I was banished until I finally accepted this fate. For no fault of my own, I was now destined to wander alone for the rest of my life or join one of the many small nomadic mage societies that wandered throughout the wilder parts of the realm. I was never truly alone, as Eamon quickly took me as his apprentice. He spent eight years teaching me how to control my heart's fire, hone my skills in magic wielding, and earn my new surname, as was tradition for mages: Fireheart.

His lessons ended abruptly a year ago when the old man passed. It was peaceful, at least, and he deserved nothing less. His passing left me with no purpose. So, I filled the lack of his presence the only way I knew how—fire wielding. If I were busy honing my skills, I would be too preoccupied to notice how quiet the world around me had become.

But now, even fire-wielding was leaving me. Over the past month, I have been steadily losing feeling in my hands. The numbness began with aching joints in my fingers, which felt swollen and clumsy, though showed no outward sign of damage. I pushed through the pain until my magic stopped working as well.

Eamon's first lesson to wielding heart's magic was to be one with yourself. You had to feel every limb your magic traveled through and be in tune with your body's condition for transference to be successful. I lost that crucial ability with the loss of feeling in my fingers. I threw myself even harder into training, sometimes going entire days without rest. Yet the harder I tried, the harder I failed.

With my emotions numb along with my hands, I dropped where I was standing before the metal target and stared at the thick canopy far above me. What was I supposed to do now? All I had in this world was Eamon and my magic. Eamon was gone, and now I was losing my magic.

What glimpses of blue sky I could see through the canopy slowly melted into hues of orange and pink as the sun dipped below a horizon I couldn't see. Orange faded into purple, which darkened to a deep blue, finally giving way to the black of night.

Alone with nothing but my memories, I spent hours filtering through them. Eamon and I would watch the night sky on nights like these. He would tell old tales of the mages before us, how different the world used to be, and all the places we could travel to if we ever decided to leave our little hovel in the woods.

A sudden realization has me sitting up quickly with a gasp. When telling tales of the wandering mage tribes, Eamon told me that if I ever found myself alone and in danger, I was to seek out the wandering mages of the Sable Desert. He claimed that no matter the circumstance, these mages would aid me in my troubles. Losing the function of my magic seemed a problem worthy of seeking out help. Besides, with Eamon gone, what was there to stop me from picking up and leaving?

I packed what few items held sentimentality or purpose the following day and set off. Remembering the directions Eamon had forced me to repeat until I could recite them in my sleep, I headed west.

Four days of travel through the Moonshire Forest brought me to the base of the Fang Mountains, aptly named for their sharp, spire-like summits. Travel through the forest had been quiet and uneventful, giving me hope for the remainder of my travels. Those hopes were smothered in my trek through the numerous passes within the Fang Mountains. The rough and rocky terrain gave little way for vegetation, and my food and water supply dwindled quickly. Though I itched to call upon my fire, I preserved my energy for the journey. Harnessing magic requires a staggering amount of energy and concentration, leaving its user physically and mentally exhausted.

A whole week after leaving my tiny home in the forest, I finally emerged from the mountains and onto the Great Ocean Prairie, named for the tall grasses that swayed in the wind like waves on the ocean. Grateful to be free of the mountains, I continue my journey westward.

After hours of walking through the ocean of waving grass, I feel like I am in a dream. The world is quiet and peaceful. The sound of the wind howling through the grass is constant and soothing. On the second day, I notice that I have gained a few traveling companions in the form of coyotes, who stalk me for two more days. Eventually, they make their move.

High-pitched yelps shatter the silence of the night—their haunting songs of the hunt echo across the open plains. The first few yips are joined by more from behind me. Within seconds, a whole choir has joined in, surrounding me on all sides.

I initially thought I was safely hidden within the confines of the tall grass. As they close in on my location, I realize that I am the one at a disadvantage. In the muted light of the moon, I can hardly see more than a foot in front of me. Coyotes don't need sight to hunt, as I'm sure the stench of my fear is enough to paint a picture for them.

Hairs tingle on the back of my neck, and I follow my gut feeling, jumping to the side as one of the hunters lunges for me. Following my instinct, I call forth my fire without thought or concentration. Considering my recent failures, I should have known it wouldn't work. To my utter surprise and relief, fire busts forth from my upraised arms, nearly blinding me as the flames illuminate my surroundings.

Horror-induced nausea crawls up my stomach as I see dozens of eyes surrounding me, reflecting the light of the flames. They do not scatter, as I hoped they would, though they do halt their advance. With a break in my concentration, my flames sputter and disappear, again plunging me into darkness. Silence coagulates around me as I realize the coyote's yips and cries have halted.

My heart pulses rapidly, and I wonder briefly if the hunters can hear it. A single yip sounds near me, and I startle, twisting toward the sound. A second later, another answers from a little father. Within seconds, the night is alive with their cries once again.

Praying to deities I had never believed in, I spread my arms toward the sky once more, calling forth my fire. Surprising me again, the flames burst forth. The last thing I want is to catch the ocean of grass around me on fire, so I keep my arms raised above the level of the vegetation and swing my arms wildly. Yips of alarm answer my flames. One lunges towards me again, and I intercept them with my fire. The smell of burnt fur accompanies the hunter's yips of pain as it darts back into the grass. The pack must finally decide I am not worth the measly meat on my bones as they retreat. No sooner does the last of my energy dissipate, and I drop to my knees.

I don't remember falling asleep after that encounter, but I must have, for the next thing I know, I am forcing my eyes open to the blinding sun. Although miraculously unharmed, I am utterly exhausted. My limbs try to resist my demands to rise and continue west, but persistence wins, and I am finally moving again. Well, perhaps stumbling is a more apt description.

Once I've found food and a small stream to replenish my water skeins, I try calling forth my fire again. Despite my success last night, not even my palms feel the warmth of my power now.

Over the next two days, the tall grasses of the prairie grow sparse. I find fewer and fewer sources of water and food, and I spend one last night on the border between the prairies and the Sable Desert. Despite the hardships I had faced on my journey, this last leg was quite possibly the most dangerous. I can only hope I am heading in the right direction when I set out the following dawn.

Four days. The last of my food disappeared on the second day—the final drop of water on the third. My skin feels so dry that I wonder if it has been flaking off to join the burning sands that rise in great dunes all around me. Just as I wandered through a gentle ocean of grass before, I now was lost in a raging sea of sand. I spent days that were so hot under the scorching sun that I could not remember what it felt like to be cold, only to find the nights so cold that I just as well could not remember the feel of the sun.

On the fifth day, I came to terms with my fate. I had lost my family and childhood home. I lost Eamon. I lost my magic. I lost my little hovel in the woods. And now, I would lose my life. I must have fallen at some point, as I am suddenly staring at the sun above me. Ironically, my last sight would be a burning ball of fire, the very element that refused to appear when summoned.

Cool water washes over me, shocking me awake. When had I fallen asleep? Dazed and confused, I try to sit up, grunting with the effort.

"Shhh. Calm, boy. Stay down. You're not quite ready to be up yet. Sleep. Rest."

The woman's voice is distant, though I can tell she is beside me as a cool hand touches my forehead. I attempt to pry my eyes open, only accomplishing a squint too blurry to reveal the speaker before darkness retakes me.

I wake again an indeterminable amount of time later to the sound of rushing water. With great effort, I manage to open my eyes. After blinking and clearing my vision, I stare at tall, strange-looking trees. The leaves are flat, possibly longer than I am tall, and all grouped at the top of a large, thin trunk. Round, hair-covered fruit the likes I've never seen before grow in clusters beneath the leaves.

Gingerly, I manage to sit up and take in my surroundings. I spy the source of the rushing water, a large creek rushing past a few feet from where I sit; its water is as clear as crystal. Dotted throughout the area are more of these strange trees. Spaced between the trees are tents of nearly every color. The sight reminds me of colorful carpets hanging on lines to dry. Men, women, and children mill about between the tents, dressed in clothing as bright as their tents.

"About time, boy. I know I told you to rest, but I didn't think you would sleep for three more days!"

I startle at the woman's words and turn to watch her approach. A stooped, elderly woman stands before a large cookfire. Her clothes are a mix of reds and yellow, with a lime-green sash tied around her waist. Upon her back is swathed a newborn. I can't tell if they are a boy or a girl, but they watch me with wide, curious eyes. Though her voice is stern, I can already tell the woman is kind. Deep laughing lines winkle around her eyes and mouth. Without a word, she extends her arm in my direction. Cool, clear water rises from the creek, flowing like a liquid snake toward the old woman before plunging into the waiting pot above the fire. My eyes widen with shock and recognition.

A water mage! Does that mean I found the wondering mages? Though perhaps they were the ones who found me, as my last memory is that of me upon my back, staring into the sun.

"Please." My voice is hardly more than a croak, and I realize it must have been weeks since I last spoke. There was little reason to talk with no one around to talk to. "I need your help. My magic is leaving me. I don't know what to do! Eamon Waterheart told me that you could help."

The woman seems to ponder this, putting her thumb and index finger to her chin. With the child's head bobbing behind her, the woman waddles in a circle around me. Though fully clothed, I feel exposed under her scrutiny.

"Hmmm. Leaving, you say? Tell me, do you have any symptoms?"

Nodding, I hold out my hands towards her as if the evidence of my infliction would be obvious. "Yes! My hands! I have lost feeling in them!" I spend the next hour telling her everything from Eamon's death to the first onset of pain in my hands to the eventual loss of nearly all function. She seemed particularly interested when I recounted my fight for survival against the coyotes. All the while, she listened carefully, nodding along to my story.

"I see... Yes, I know what is wrong."

I can't help but hold my breath, fearing her next words. Was I doomed? Would I never practice magic again? What would become of me then? Could I return to my childhood home? Would I even want to?

"You're overworked." With that, she returned to the large pot. She began adding vegetables and herbs to the boiling water with practiced movements.

I stare at the woman, my mouth agape. Overworked? I peer down at my hands. They are scared and covered in calluses, as one would expect of a flame wielder, but otherwise look just as they always have. I glance back at the woman, squinting.

"My hands... are... overworked? Can this be cured?"

"Yes, yes. Just overworked. It happens to the best of us, especially when we are young and motivated. You practiced magic non-stop for nearly a month. What did you expect to happen? As the smallest extremity your power has to pass through, your poor fingers tend to take the brunt of the work when directing your flames. It's quite common with fire wielders. As for a cure, you need a nice, long break, and you'll be good as new! Might I suggest the Sable Desert Oasis? It's quite beautiful this time of year." Chuckling to herself, she pulled out long strips of dried meat and tossed them into the pot.

"So... I haven't lost my magic?"

"Nope."

"Then coming all the way here was pointless?"

"Seems so. Though I'm sure it'll be a fun story to tell your children one day."

I couldn't believe it. That would explain why I could summon my flames against the coyotes. It had been over a week since I had last even tried to wield my magic, inadvertently giving my hands the chance to heal.

What energy I had left drained from me, and I plopped back onto my makeshift bed, staring again at the strange tree. Lifting my left hand above me, I stared hard at my palm, asking the woman what kind of trees these were. I couldn't help but laugh at the irony as she told me they were called palm trees.

At the woman's suggestion, who I later learned was called Abdali and is the tribe's healer, I abstained from using my heart's fire. I might have thought refraining from using my magic would be a challenge had I not been put to work as Abdali's personal workhorse. Scouring the oasis for herbs, helping the men hunt, tending to the pack mules, and hauling water were just a few of my everyday chores. I may have grumbled and complained at first, but the truth was that it felt good to belong somewhere again. For the first time since Eamon's passing, I wasn't alone.

Much to my surprise, the wandering mages of the Sable Desert were not only home to magic wielders but non-magic users as well. Hidden within the depths of the desert was a society of people I had only heard about from Eamon's stories. People of all nationalities, gifted and not, live and work alongside one another.

More fascinating still were the different types of magic wielders. Besides my own fire and Eamon's water, I had only heard the tales of other types. I never thought I would get to see them with my own eyes.

I met Windhearts, Earthhearts, Florahearts, and Faunahearts. The latter two were ones I had never heard of before. According to some elders who told stories around the nightly fires, there were even more varieties of magic wielders in the world forced into hiding.

I lived with the wandering mages for three months as they traversed the desert from one oasis to another. Respecting the land, they never stayed longer than necessary at any one location lest they rob the area of its natural resources required to sustain itself and the surrounding wildlife. On my first journey back into the sea of sand, I was nearly overcome with fear and apprehension, as my first experience had almost cost me my life. However, the wandering mages were well equipped for travel through the desert, including decades of techniques for surviving in the rough landscape that were passed down from generation to generation.

At the beginning of my stay, I would count down the days until I could test my fire-wielding again. As the weeks passed, my excitement turned into uncertainty. Once I was cured and able to wield my fire, what happened then? Would I leave the wandering mages and head back to the forests of Moonshire Wood? Would I return to the solitude of the hovel I shared with Eamon? Such thoughts kept me awake long into the night, keeping me from rest and souring my mood for the following day.

At long last, and yet far too soon, Abdali approaches me one morning to inform me that my time of rest is at it's end. Tribesmen and women gather excitedly around me, all more than familiar with my recent plight. Though I dread what the end of my ailment means for my future, their excitement is infectious, and I soon find myself at the edge of the oasis, facing an endless horizon of sand. The entirety of the tribe stands behind me, waiting on bated breath for me to wield my flames.

Bouncing on the balls of my feet, I shake out my stiff arms, hoping to shake out my anxieties as well. I stop, close my eyes, and take a deep breath, willing my mind to clear. Immediately, I feel the familiar and welcome spark of energy deep within me. Magic.

My heart leaps at the familiar sensation, and I force the emotion back lest I break my focus. Honing my attention on that spark, I urge it to grow. It heeds my command, warmth flooding my torso as it increases. Once satisfied with the energy built within my chest, I urge the fire to spread to my shoulders, then down my biceps and forearms, halting at my wrists.

I allow the magic to stop there while I take a few breaths. This is it. This is the final test. One last breath in... and out.

I push the magic further into my hands, palms burning. I want to keep my eyes closed, almost too afraid to see whether or not my flames will come when called forth. At the encouragement of the people behind me, I force them open. I move my arms forward, spread my fingers wide, and angle my palms toward the empty desert in front of me.

Finally, I push my magic towards my fingers and beyond, using the direction of my palms to direct the flow of elemental flames that should burst from me. I anticipate my fingers burning with the transference of power.

Vibrant jets of flame burst forward, the heat so intense that my hands twitch with the need to cover my face. Like a stream of pressurized water, the flames reach nearly a hundred feet away from me before lapping at the sandy earth. Elated, I try to keep the blaze going for as long as possible. Over the roar of the flames, I can barely make out the crowd's cheers behind me.

When I can stand the strain no longer, I allow the flames to die out. As the heat dissipates, I slump to my knees, laughing. I did it! My magic was back! And now that it was back, I could... what? Go home? Where even was my home? Would the wandering mages expect me to pick up and leave now that I was healed?

A hard whack to the back of my head breaks me from my spiraling thoughts.

"What's wrong with you, Soren?" With my hand rubbing the sore spot on the back of my head, I turn to see Abdali standing behind me, a rolled palm leaf in her hand. "Haven't you learned your lesson already? You only just recovered from overworking your poor body, and then you go and turn half the dessert into glass! I hope you enjoyed your little show, for you'll have to rest for at least another week before I let you so much as light a campfire!" With a harrumph, she places her gnarled hands on her hips. "How are you supposed to start taking on the fireheart chores from now on if you can't be trusted to use your own magic?"

Despite her chastising, my heart skipped at her words. "From now on, Abdali?"

Her glower softened, the laughing lines around her eyes and mouth lifting in a soft smile. "Yes, Soren. From now on. Or was there someplace else you needed to be?"

"No," my voice broke as tears stung at the corners of my eyes. I quickly rubbed them away before anyone could see. "No,

Abdali. Where else would I go? This is… my home."

"Yes, it is." From my position on my knees, she had no trouble placing a hand on my head, patting it as I'd seen her do with the crowd of children who often followed her around. "This is your home. And just like everyone else, you must help care for it. Now," she whacked me again with the rolled palm leaf, although this time a bit lighter. "Off with you! The water isn't going to haul itself."

Chuckling, I stood, dusting hot sand from my knees. Something sharp snagged one of my sleeves, and I winced. Upon closer inspection, I found shards of glass embedded in the knees of my trousers. From the base of my feet reaching nearly one hundred feet out into the desert, a shimmering line of glass marked the passing of my flames.

The power of my Fireheart.

The Covenant of Redemption

The Blasphemer. A figure unfathomably grotesque, wreathed in an eldritch glow. Too many eyes but not enough heads. Too many fingers but not enough hands. A waking nightmare of elder corruption. It stalks the land, with only whispers and desolation left in its wake. Villages and towns, where only days before were full of life, are now devoid of all traces. Homes, storefronts, and farms are left rotted and defunct as if the people who lived there not a fortnight before hadn't existed for a decade.

The smell of sulfur and copper permeated the air, suffocating, like a heavy fog brought into Trainwin Harbor by the early fall wind despite it being the dead of winter. Renald pulled off his silver helm, uncomfortably stifling in the unnatural vapor, and shifted anxiously in his half plate. Even his noble sensibility was suppressed by the cloying brimstone in the air.

Alandra's lithe silhouette appeared a few feet away as she finished inspecting the red-charred remains of some humanoid leaning against a shattered shopkeep's window.

A voice deep and gruff, yet booming, shattered the eerie quiet of the street. "Well? What are we going to do now?"

Alandra shot the diminutive, stocky man a withering glare. Her voice was barely above a whisper, more akin to a hiss.

"Handon, could you *not* do that, please?"

The blue-tattooed dwarf moved his weight from one armored foot to the other, passing his warhammer between his hands. Seeing the dwarven warrior anxious made Renald feel better for his own disquiet.

Handon bristled at the tall, elven woman. "I don't like this, I cann'ae see my hand in front of my face."

"Where is Walleria?" Renald asked, causing the dwarf in front of him to jump. He hadn't noticed the paladin standing just a few feet behind.

Alandra waved her hand dismissively toward the building across the street as she knelt over the remains. "You know how clerics of Aelin are. She's probably blessing the dead or saying a prayer."

The paladin nodded and left the dwarven warrior and elven ranger alone to bicker, as they were known to do. The bickering between the two could last for days. Renald had learned long ago that any intervention between the two was futile. He couldn't remember any of their arguments yielding a victor, only ending when another reason to quarrel presented itself, the topic of the previous disagreement all but forgotten.

He found Walleria in the crumbled structure of what may have been a family home. The cleric was staring down at the remains of a small family, red-charred as all the others they had found. Two large bodies were huddled together over the forms of two smaller figures. Parents futilely protecting their children.

Bile rose quickly, the paladin having to swallow the nausea back lest the contents of his stomach desecrate the remnants of the small harbor town. Walleria, her small frame hunched over the family's remains, stared unseeing, her eyes half-lidded.

Renald could hardly hear her whispered prayers, even standing beside the small woman. He waited patiently for her to finish.

"I know what you want to ask me." Her words, usually soft and filled with kindness, were strained. "And I cannot give you the answer you desire."

"People are going to keep dying unless we do something. Following in the aftermath, burying the dead and sending prayers to the gods. That is all well and good. Noble, even. But it changes nothing."

The cleric sighed and stood to her full height, which only reached the paladin's armored chest. She looked exhausted. They all were. Tired of the chase, tired of the hopelessness. The silence drew out between them as they surveyed the destruction around them. The only sound breaking the unnerving quiet was the hum of the other two members of their party, still bickering, and the distant splash of waves breaking upon the docks. Finally, the small woman spoke.

"I just need more time."

"Walleria, it's been three years. Time is a commodity that is quickly running out, and if we don't -"

"I will not act against my faith." Her reply was sharp, taking Renald by surprise, only to be quickly replaced by fury.

"You think this is a request I make *lightly?*" He kept his voice lowered, both out of respect for the recently deceased and to keep his anger in check. "This act alone will be the cause of my excommunication, earn divine disfavor from not only Aelin but all deities, and not to mention damn my soul."

"Then how can you make such a demand, knowing the consequences?"

"Because my soul is not worth the lives of thousands." Renald could feel the heat of his anger creeping up his neck. To avoid further argument and perhaps saying something he might come to regret, he turned before Walleria could respond and marched away. His other companions had moved away from the destroyed buildings and were readying their horses. He avoided their questioning stares and instead mounted his destrier. Without another word, the rest of the party mounted, including the cleric, who had followed behind Renald and made their way out of the town and along the coast.

For three years, the party had been hunting this abomination. Stemmed from the darkest depths of whatever hell it had crawled from, the demon was challenging to track. Despite the devastation it left in its wake, there was never a clear path or trail left behind. It just simply vanished. Days, even weeks – and on a few occasions, months – would pass before another destroyed settlement was found.

In an act of desperation, the four nations of the realm had come together to strike an accord. The Men of Telnora, the Dwarves of Echerspire, the Elven of Mironwood, and the Halflings of Davenshire.

Through a series of tests and championships, each race selected a hero of their people. By joining the different races, each party member would represent their homeland's contribution to the pact and provide a unique talent to aid the party's quest. To hunt down and destroy the entity released upon their realm by any means necessary. Thus, the four were brought together.

Alandra, the Elven Ranger. Handon, the Dwarven Warrior. Renald, the Human Paladin. And Walleria, the Halfling Cleric. With differences ranging from speech, diet, and religion, the first few months of their fellowship were a challenge to not only decide upon a plan to defeat the demon but also how to complete their quest without destroying each other in the process.

Three years into their travels, they had learned not only to coexist but depend on one another. Even Alandra and Handon, despite their constant quarreling, would stand back-to-back in conflict should the need arise. However, they were still just as uncertain about how they would destroy the demon as they were at the beginning. At least, they had been until their travels led them through a small town in the swamp that bordered the lands of halflings and dwarves.

Their discovery of the small village was complete happenstance, as their initial destination had been an informant in the dwarven city of Kallidor. What buildings had once existed were no more than husks of their former selves. Charred and decaying bodies littered the gravel roads between clusters of ruins. Sulfur and brimstone hung heavy in the thick, humid air. The Blasphemer had come through this village, leaving little to nothing in its wake.

During their usual inspection of the area for survivors – which there never were – or traces the demon may have left behind, Renald discovered a small temple. With what remained of the dissolving structure, the paladin found evidence of strange drawings and glyphs decorating nearly every surface still standing. None of the markings were recognizable to the paladin. They were, however, familiar to the cleric. As a woman of religion, Renald had been surprised to see her blatant disgust upon seeing his discovery. Muttering her prayers, she refused to move closer to the temple's ruins.

Two days of pestering the halfling woman revealed the source of her contempt.

"Malphion worshipers." She spat the words as though they

tasted foul. "They pray to the deities of the Abyssal Realms. What your people might call Hell."

"They worship devils?" Walleria nodded, glaring at the ground between her feet as though she could see through the surface to the offending realm itself.

The concept of devil-worshiping was not unheard of to Renald. If this were the case, he found it odd that a people who revered the deity most likely responsible for The Blasphemer's existence was not protected from its own ruination. Perhaps their prayers attracted the demon to such a remote location in the first place.

Despite the deaths and devastation the party encountered during their hunt, the Malphion Temple dwelt at the forefront of Renald's thoughts. Three years had passed, thousands of innocent lives had been lost, and they were no closer to stopping this madness than at the start. Perhaps what they needed was a deity of their own. If praying to the Gods was all it took to banish the demon, they would have done so years ago. Perhaps they were praying to the wrong gods.

Such thoughts were sacrilegious to the Paladin's Code that Renald lived by. He dismissed the idea the moment it crossed his mind, though he found himself revisiting the theory in the dark hours of the night when he found no distraction from his travels or the bickering of his companions.

A month after the party traveled through the swamp, he discussed his speculation with Walleria. Her immediate revulsion came as no shock. Her demand for him to never mention such heretical acts lest he threaten their accord, however, did surprise him. The cleric was a kind woman. She was quiet by nature, as most halflings were. To see such disdain directed at himself left Renald reeling.

He never mentioned a word of the topic to her again until the group found themselves amidst the ruins of Trainwin Harbor. This time, he refused to let the subject lapse.

Silence coagulated around the quartet, each lost in their thoughts as they set up camp for the night. Not a word had been uttered since they left the harbor. The wariness and soul-deep exhaustion Renald felt was reflected in each of his comrade's faces. He waited until they had all eaten and settled around what remained of their small cook-fire before clearing his throat.

"I have...an idea." Silence was his only response. He could feel the weight of their combined gazes. One especially burned through the top of his slightly bowed head. "This idea is... well... it is heresy at its most basic level, but it may be our only option." He raised his head to look at each of his companions in turn. "We cannot allow any more people to die because of our incompetence."

Alandra and Handon met him with curious stares. Walleria sighed and stood, pacing to their tethered horses and picking up a brush.

"What are ye goin' on about?" Handon. Gruff and to the point, as always.

"We've prayed to the Gods, and they are either not answering us or are incapable of rendering aid. Perhaps we should try praying to a different deity."

Elven eyebrows raised, dwarven eyes narrowed, and a halfling scoffed from where she stood brushing down her horse. "He wants to pray to Malphion."

"Who is Malphion?" Renald opened his mouth to answer Alandra's question. Handon beat him to it.

"You want to pray to a bloody devil? Are you insane, boy?"

"It may be our only choice. Do you have any other ideas? Because I would love to hear them."

"And what makes you believe that this devil, this…Malphion would help?" To her credit, Alandra sounded genuinely curious rather than accusatory. "I may not be familiar with the gods of men, but devils are not known for answering prayers out of the kindness of their hearts."

Renald took a deep, steadying breath. "Of course not. But they might be willing to make a trade. A deal, even."

"And what could you offer a devil? It's a bloody devil!" Handon scoffed and shook his head.

"My soul."

Stunned silence settled over the campsite. Even Walleria had stopped brushing her horse, staring at Renald with wide eyes. He waited for someone to say something, anything. Instead, they all stared with combined expressions of fear and confusion.

"If this works, if Malphion will take my soul in exchange for the banishment of his demon, then I will happily make the exchange. What is one life when faced with the possible annihilation of thousands? I intend to make this deal… with or without your consent. I will return to the Malphion Temple we found in the swamps first thing in the morning."

Without another word, the paladin stood, retrieved his sword beside his bedroll, and stalked into the night to take the first watch.

****

The following morning, the fog hung thick between the trees as Renald saddled his horse. He had yet to speak to any of his companions, though they each were up as well, readying their mounts. It was better this way. He had never been one for goodbyes. Mounting his steed, he headed west.

The songs of morning birds cut through the thick fog alongside the clopping of his steeds' massive hooves. A minute later, the familiar sound of multiple hooves trampling through the thin foliage joined in. Behind his helm, Renald smiled as an elf, dwarf, and halfling fell in step behind him.

****

With her hands on her hips, Alandra finally broke the silence and asked the same question on everyone's mind. "What now?"

They stood at the base of the remains of Malphion's Temple. The four exchanged unsure glances before settling on Walleria. Her face was sickly and pale, her hands wringing themselves before her. Noticing the attention, she shrugged.

"Similar to how you'd pray to any other deity, I suppose."

No one moved as their attention returned to the temple. Finally, Renald took the first step. He removed his armor, took one last deep breath, then stepped into the large circle etched into the floor and surrounded by strange glyphs. He stole one last glance at his companions – no, his friends – before closing his eyes.

"In the name of the Abyssal Plane, I invoke the deity Malphion. Hear my prayer."

Frogs croaked. A bird called in the distance. A swarm of gnats buzzed annoyingly close. Renald resisted the urge to swat them away. The buzz of the swarm grew louder, unpleasant vibrations echoing down the paladin's spine. Able to stand it no longer, he opened his eyes and slapped at the swarm hovering before him. Before his eyes, the swarm grew, became darker, and began to take shape. Long, pitch-black arms ending with hooked fingers extended from the mob of insects, followed by a bare, featureless chest. Lastly, a massive,

133

horned head formed. Eyes as red as glowing embers peered back out at the speechless group.

Renald's first instinct was to recoil and draw his sword. He commanded his body to do so but only found himself rooted to the spot. He was unsure whether his fear or some other nefarious entity held him in place. Eyes awash in the hues of fresh blood settled on the paladin. When the devil spoke, each group member flinched, for it was not the sound of a single voice that reached their ears but the chorus of thousands. Men, women, and children alike spoke as one.

"As summoned, I have come. What reason would a pious soldier such as yourself have for this summons? You are not my child; your prayers are not mine to receive. Curiosity only is the reason for my compliance. Be it that your reasoning is warranted, and I may allow you to continue your meager existence."

Renald's breath caught as he opened his mouth to reply. How did one speak to a god? Or a devil? Should he bow and act reverent? The mere thought of showing supplication to this dark being caused his stomach to roil.

"Malphion, I come to you not as your child but as a child of this realm regardless. An entity is loose in our realm. A being not of our world, we cannot destroy it. It has claimed hundreds of innocent lives."

The horned beast sneered in response. "I am aware of my creation's behaviors."

Renald bit his tongue to keep his face expressionless, a feat he was sure he was not accomplishing. "We implore you to return this entity to your world, lest it deplete ours of life. I…" He swallowed back the bile, threatening to rise. "I am willing to trade my soul for this service."

Crimson orbs considered this, looking so deeply into Renald that he felt the entity could see directly into the soul he was offering, determining its value.

"You consider your single paltry soul enough compensation?" His heart dropped. He hadn't considered the possibility of his offer being denied.

"Not just his soul." Walleria stepped into the circle of the temple alongside him. Renald wanted to push her away but refrained. "Mine as well."

"Aye." Handon and Alandra stepped within the temple as well. The devil eyed them each, as he had done with Renald. The few moments of contemplation that passed felt eternal to the quartet. At long last, the sneer on the deity's features spread to a satisfied grin.

"It will be done, and shall your souls know no escape from this accord."

Watchers

The asylum's security surveillance room was a claustrophobic chamber adorned with peeling wallpaper, crumbling shelves stacked with aged records, a small wooden desk, and an uncomfortable metal chair that creaked under the most minute amount of weight. A single rotary dial telephone sat on the desk. A thick layer of dust covered every surface but the desk and chair. The dim overhead lightbulb flickered sporadically, casting eerie shadows across the aging linoleum floor that peeled in the corners.

The centerpiece of this dilapidated room was a massive wall lined with outdated, grayscale CCTV monitors. Each monitor displayed a different section of the asylum—a haunting panorama of deserted hallways, medical examination rooms furnished with rusting metal beds and equipment, large dining areas, office spaces, and various other rooms possibly used for forms of recreation.

The monitors were ancient relics of a bygone era. Their screens emitted a faint, sickly glow that exaggerated the shadows lurking in the room's corners. The images displayed were grainy, distorted, and pixelated. A small hand-written label accompanied each screen, indicating the location of the video feed. The cameras themselves, once cutting-edge technology, were now obsolete and barely functional, occasionally losing connection for a few seconds at a time.

The crackling audio of static from the occasional disconnected video feeds added to the eerie ambiance. It was as if the very essence of the asylum had seeped into the wires and circuits, imbuing an unsettling presence into the surveillance system.

James was two hours into his new job and already regretted accepting the position. As a college dropout struggling to make ends meet, the job posting for a part-time security surveillance officer with great pay was almost too good to be true. No certifications or education were required to apply; the agency didn't even require any previous experience. The pay was nearly double the current minimum wage. The only downside to the posting had been the hours; from nine o'clock at night until five in the morning.

James was surprised he was the only one to accept the position after the interview. Unwilling to let such a good-paying opportunity pass, he agreed to all the terms he was presented during his interview and had no follow-up questions when asked. As such, he was hired on the spot and given the time and address of his first shift.

Looking back, James realized he should have asked at least a few questions, such as where he would be working and why no one else had accepted the position following the interview.

Lunaria Sanitarium, built in 1920, was nestled deep within the forests of the Pacific Northwest. Portland, Oregon, was the nearest city, taking at least an hour and a half by car. The hospital consisted of three separate buildings. The central four-story building contained medical rooms, recreational suites, and other administrative offices. Each two-story wing building housed bedrooms with minimal furniture, a dining hall with rows of tables and chairs, and basements with locked holding rooms. Only the hallway leading to the doors for the holding rooms contained a camera in each basement.

Every room in the sanitarium still contained original furniture from when it was abandoned, as if all inhabitants had left for the day and never returned. Vacated in the late 50's, the entire property was left untouched for nearly seven decades. Courtyards, fields, and small farming patches were overgrown, nearly reclaimed by the forest whose land it was built upon. Despite the impending vegetation, the buildings were surprisingly in good condition despite the rust, mold, and rotting surfaces.

Upon relieving the daytime officer at nine o'clock, a gangly older man who did not explain his duties other than not to fall asleep, James settled in for a long night. The metal chair behind the desk protested against his weight, and he made a mental note to bring a cushion for his next shift. Figuring he would need help staying awake and being kept from boredom, James brought a backpack stocked with snacks, energy drinks, his hand-held gaming console, and a few books his sister had lent him. He debated whether he would get in trouble for playing games or reading while on duty. But how hard could watching screens of empty rooms be? Surely, he would get in more trouble for falling asleep rather than being partially distracted.

Gaze darting between monitors on the wall before him, unease settled deep within his gut. The screens were grainy and out of focus, an occasional ripple in the feed giving the effect of movement and catching his attention. The wall of monitors was so wide that he had trouble viewing every screen without turning his head, causing the screens on the opposite side to disappear from his focus completely.

As the minutes ticked by with no changes, James relaxed and pulled his gaming console from his pack. He kept the volume low, just in case, and was careful to peek at the screens between each level of his game. The few games he owned that didn't require an internet connection quickly lost his interest. He glanced at the time on his cell phone. Ten thirty. An hour and a half into his shift, he was already bored.

As James reached for his backpack, a scratchy static sound caught his attention. One of the screens in the top row, labeled "East Wing Dining Hall," showed nothing but black, gray, and white interference. Heart leaping into his throat, James watched as the lines danced across the screen. Less than a handful of seconds later, the feed resumed, and he was presented again with long rows of tables and chairs. Breathing a sigh of relief, James slumped back into his chair, the metal groaning in protest. Waiting for his heart rate to settle, James took in the creepy aspects of the dining hall showing through the feed.

Long, wooden tables made up a majority of the space. Looking to be made of one solid piece of wood, James could only imagine how heavy they must be. Chairs dotted the spaces between the tables, all pulled out and looked haphazardly pushed around, a few even lying on their sides. A single door in the far-left corner of the room stood open, leading to the hallway beyond.

James's attention fixated on the chairs. Had they been pushed out from the tables before? Racking his memory, he thought they had been pushed in, not that he had paid particular attention to the small details. Clearing his thoughts with a shake, he pulled one of his energy drinks out and popped the cap. Perhaps he just remembered wrong.

While sipping the carbonated liquid energy, James pulled out a notebook and pen and began taking notes on the condition of each room, more for the peace of his own mind and to pass the time than any other reason.

MAIN BUILDING

Lobby
Large circular desk
Rows of wheelchairs – neatly stacked
Multiple couches and chairs
Rows of gurneys against the back wall
Office Staff Rooms (all the same)
Desk
Chair
Filing cabinet – drawers closed
Door closed
Medical Examination Rooms (all the same)
Patient bed
Large table
Desk
Chair
Cabinet – closed
Door closed
Recreation Rooms (all the same)
Two couches
Three recliners
One large table in the center with chairs pushed in
Two small tables
Shelves with books put away
Door closed

EAST WING
Bedrooms (all the same)
Bed
Small desk and chair – pushed in
Small wardrobe – drawers closed
Door closed
Dining Hall
Rows of large tables
Chairs not pushed in
Door open
Basement
All doors closed
WEST WING
Bedrooms (all the same)
Bed
Small desk and chair – pushed in
Small wardrobe – drawers closed
Door closed
Dining Hall
Rows of large tables
Chairs pushed in
Door closed
Basement
All doors closed

He hadn't realized before just how uniform and orderly every room was for a mental hospital that was supposedly abandoned. The only monitors he did not make notes on were the ones facing outside, towards the overgrown courtyards and fields.

Satisfied, James rechecked the time. Eleven o'clock. Two hours down, six more to go. He flipped to a fresh page in his notebook and started another list, this time with ideas of items to bring to help pass the time and fend off boredom. He also jotted down a note to research why this place had been abandoned and to inquire with his employer why there was a need for 24-hour surveillance.

Blaring static caused James to jump and nearly knock what remained of his energy drink off the desk. Another camera feed had disconnected, and this one was labeled to be in the main building inside of a staff office. He waited for the static to clear, holding his breath. Just as before, the picture resumed after only a few seconds. His sigh of relief lodged in his throat, nearly causing him to cough. The filing cabinets were all open.

Breathless, James stared at the screen. Had the cabinets been open before? He could have sworn they were closed. With shaking hands, he flipped through the pages of his notebook until he came across the description for that camera feed.

Filing cabinets – drawers closed.

Standing, James reached up and tapped on the screen showing the office, as though this act would either close the drawers or fix the feed to reflect what he had jotted down in his notebook. Of course, neither of those happened.

James lost track of how long he stood, staring at the screen, unable to develop a cohesive thought. The sound of static blared once again. He flinched so violently that he nearly lost his footing. Bracing himself on the desk before him, James watched in dawning terror as another screen fizzled with black, grey, and white lines. The label under the monitor read "West Wing Basement Hallway."

When the image cleared, James kept his eyes focused on the label, too afraid to see what change might have happened this time. In a hallway containing only doors, it wasn't hard to guess. Slowly, he lifted his gaze and confronted the screen. A door halfway down the hall was standing wide open.

James could not see into the room from the camera angle, something he was immensely grateful for. He did not need to reference his notes this time. He knew the doors had all been closed before.

Sitting heavily in the chair, James ran a clammy hand down his face. He could do little more than stare at the screen and focus on breathing. Once his panic had settled slightly, he reached for his cell phone, intending to call his employer. The time showed twenty-four minutes past midnight as he tried to navigate toward the email that contained emergency contact numbers. He nearly slammed his phone on the desk as he realized he had no signal this far out into the forest.

Snatching up the receiver of the old rotary dial telephone on the desk, James spared only a second to thank his mother's love of old movies for providing the knowledge of how to use such a relic. This knowledge proved for naught as the phone, though wired into the wall, provided no dial tone. The line was dead.

Movement from one of the central screens startled him. He dropped the metal receiver, its impact on the wooden desk much too loud for the small, cramped room, causing him to flinch again. James frantically scanned the monitors, trying to find the source of the movement. All the screens showed their respective feeds, with none having lost connection or being filled with static.

James forced a few deep breaths, though this did nothing to ease the panicked sickness rising from his stomach and up his throat. His hands, though cold, sweated profusely. He rubbed his palms on his jeans as he began pacing the small room. He had half a mind to leave. What was the worst that would happen? He could get fired. With how these first few hours played out, being fired and never returning to this place again wasn't much of a deterrent.

The small room housing the security surveillance was in a small stand-alone building that used to be a shed. Located just off the main entry road and only a few steps from the entrance to the main building, it would be all too easy to step outside, hop in his car, and leave this place far behind.

Static. James froze mid-stride toward his backpack. Another feed had disconnected. This time, the label indicated the camera was in the main lobby. He waited once again with bated breath for the camera to reconnect. Once the screen reappeared, a whimper broke from him before he could stop it.

The wheelchairs, previously placed in neat rows along the far wall, were scattered throughout the lobby. Most were still standing on their wheels. Others looked like they were thrown or kicked over, resting either on their sides or completely upside down. The few gurneys, previously against the other wall, were knocked over or shoved on the lobby receptionist's desk. The large, double doors leading to the front courtyard stood wide open.

James would only need to open the door to his surveillance room and turn to the right to see the open doors of the institution. All thoughts of leaving the safety of his tiny room fled.

Within seconds, another feed dropped, the room filling with the harsh static sound again. Before James could look to read the label, another monitor flickered abruptly to black, grey, and white fizzled lines. Then another, until every single screen lost connection with its corresponding camera.

As abruptly as it began, the first feed to disconnect refreshed again. The bedroom on the screen was in complete disarray. Sheets were shredded and tossed about the space. The wardrobe's drawers were pulled free of their frame, the empty containers tossed haphazardly around. The small desk was cracked down in its center.

The screen jolted back to static as another feed cleared. This time, it was a medical examination room. Cabinets were torn open, and equipment was strewn about the space. Surgical tools were embedded in the furniture and walls. Before James could observe anything else, another screen cleared, pulling his attention.

All doors in the basement hallways of both Wings were open. One was still swinging on its hinges as though whatever influence opened the door had done so with force.

Every monitor flickered between static and clear video feed so quickly that James could do little more than see snippets before the feed was either disconnected or his attention was drawn to another screen. Every room was in complete disarray, the level of destruction changing each time the feed fizzled out and returned.

The single fluorescent light in the ceiling of his small room surged brightly before shattering, pitching the room into eerie darkness only interrupted by the flashing black and white of the camera feeds.

The scratching noise of static became more than James could bear. He longed to run, but terror held him in place. Having unconsciously backed into a corner of the room, he buried his head beneath his arms, trying desperately to cut out the sound of the static. He wanted to scream, though he wasn't sure if perhaps he already was, as nothing could be heard over the interference.

Huddled on the floor, James peeked between his arms at the wall of monitors flickering in and out of connection. He thought he saw movement in a monitor as it reflected a room a few times, though the connection was cut too soon for him to tell.

All at once, every monitor but the middlemost fizzled to static and did not reconnect. James could not distinguish the screen's contents from his huddled position in the corner, though he could tell something was different. Working up what smidgen of courage remained, he unfolded from himself and crawled forward until he could see the details of the screen.

A small room containing a single desk, a metal chair, a few shelves, and a large wall of static screens was shown. A figure was on their hands and knees in the middle of the room, gazing toward the wall of monitors.

James was looking at himself. The view of the screen would place the camera directly behind him, in the corner adjacent to where he huddled earlier. He did not have to turn and look to know there were no cameras in the surveillance room.

Too afraid to tear his eyes from the screen, it fizzled to static for only a fraction of a second before clearing again. The screen was the same, except for another figure standing behind James in the corner he had occupied only seconds before.

A scream louder than the static ripped from James's throat as he lurched forward and away from the entity. He grabbed his half-open backpack and sprinted for the door without a glance or second thought. Ice-cold air stung his lungs and chilled his tear-streaked cheeks as he bolted for his car. Gravel and dirt flew from spinning tires as he sped away from the institute.

Unable to resist, James glanced in the rearview mirror. Next to the open double doors of the main building stood a figure shrouded in darkness, watching the retreating form of his car disappear into the forest.

Enkindled

The gate is weakening.
　　Hush. He still has time.
　　He hears us now. See how he flinches?
Yes, but he still has time. We must have patience.

Eldric paused in his task, allowing his trembling hands to set the fist-sized lump of wood on top of the pile of completed figurines. Creating the small talismans was usually easy and required little to no thought. For some reason, he couldn't figure out how to finish his most recent creation. The voices were only making it more difficult.

Out of habit alone, he glanced toward the eastern wall of the cavern where a pile of stone slabs lay. Each slab, roughly the size of a tome, was etched with hundreds of jagged tally marks. He had stopped keeping track of the passing days long ago, sometime after completing the twentieth tab. He figured at least two decades had passed since his watch began, but how long ago had he stopped counting? Months? Years, perhaps? Decades? He wasn't sure the years he had counted were even accurate as it was impossible to gauge the passing of time within the depths of The Dark.

Becoming the next Keeper was a dream of nearly every child. The Keepers held higher praise than even the Pantheon, as they alone kept The Dark at bay. Though this knowledge was common, few knew the technicalities of what a Keeper's duties entailed. Very few. And those few individuals who did know went to great lengths to ensure no one knew the truth.

For decades, Eldric had served as the Keeper. Even he did not know the truth. For his bravery and extraordinary prowess on the battlefield, he had been chosen to ascend to the position. No privilege could be higher, especially for one as young as he had been, hardly past the cusp of manhood.

Even after years in darkness, Eldric could still remember the swelling pride in his chest as he was led from the ranks and into the Temple of the Light. Few were allowed to walk the halls of the Pantheon, the Keeper being one of those few. Pride and unwavering determination to prove himself worthy of the title kept the boy from asking any questions surrounding his new duties, sure that the Priests of The Light would not have chosen him if there was any doubt in his abilities.

Miles beneath the Temple, after traversing numerous tunnels and shafts in near complete darkness, Eldric was at last shown his post and provided instruction.

Keep the Flame alive, for it is the Flame that holds The Dark at bay.

That was all he was told before he was left alone deep within the stone, miles below the surface, with only a burning brazier, a single bedroll, and piles of wood and supplies that were mysteriously replenished during the scant hours Eldric allowed himself to sleep.

With no other instruction given to him, Eldric did as he was tasked. He kept the Flame alive.

The pocket of space deep within the ground that had become his home was just that. At his back, a jagged crack in the stone-faced wall spanned from the ground to the ceiling a mere five feet above his head. Slate walls lined the small cavern on each side, eventually disappearing before him past the border of light emitted from the Flame, which roared strongly in a metal brazier in the center of the floor.

The only warning he had received upon taking up his post, besides not letting the Flame flicker or go out, was to stay within the protection of the light.

Eldric began keeping a tally of the passing days less than a week into his solitude. Having no sun or stars to indicate the passage of time, he measured the days by the frequency at which he slept. He only slept when his wood and food storage became low. From the onset, he knew his method was flawed and likely inaccurate. However, he continued the habit for the sake of his sanity.

One month into his duty as Keeper, he began carving figurines into the wood he was supplied to feed the Flame. The whittling was an attempt to keep himself busy to avoid looking into the depths of The Dark just past the lit border of the Flame. At first, the carvings were figures of people he knew. His mother. What he could remember of his father, who had died in a border skirmish when he was only a child. His best friend. The girl he loved and would someday marry when his duty was done.

He no longer entertained such frivolous fantasies. He had known upon accepting this post that his duty wouldn't end. In recorded history, there had never been a Keeper who returned from their post. Even now, decades later, he continued to carve the figures, though he did not know who he a-likened them to. Perhaps they were people he once knew. Perhaps not.

Years passed in this manner until Eldric stopped avoiding the darkness around him, dropping all pretense that the ominous presence didn't exist. Not for a moment during his solitude did he feel truly alone. There was something there, just beyond the reaches of the Flame. He didn't know what – or who – was there, but he could feel their presence. When he finally acknowledged that he was not alone in the abyss, he stopped tallying the days, and the concept of time ceased to exist.

Some time ago, Eldric wasn't sure how long as he had forgotten how to do such calculations, the whispering began. Having forgotten the sound of another's voice, Eldric had at first been startled, nearly calling out into the darkness beyond the crevasse in the wall behind him. He realized then that he no longer had a voice. How long had it been since he had spoken? He couldn't remember. One did not speak to The Dark, which had been his sole companion for longer than he could remember.

The whispers gradually grew louder, new voices joining in the chorus. They called to him in the beginning, excitement evident in their tones. As Eldric ignored them, they turned accusatory, insulted by his lack of response. They no longer vied for his attention, instead speaking amongst themselves, discussing the progress of his insanity as though his breaking point was an event they eagerly awaited.

Hands trembling, chest pounding, he could take the torment no longer. Tossing the unfinished figurine he'd been struggling with into a basket, Eldric stood and faced The Dark. He wanted to shout, to yell into the abyss and vent his frustration. He opened his mouth, and only the strangled garb of vocal cords left unused for far too long emerged.

He finally speaks!

Well, he tries. He does not yet realize we can hear him, even if he does not speak.

Does this mean it is time?

The voices raised in volume, talking over one another in excitement.

Yes! It is time!

The Rebirth is upon us!

We do not know yet what he will do. This may be The End.

It is time!

The Rebirth!

Eldric slammed his hands against his ears, trying desperately to block out the voices. The sudden crescendo was overwhelming. Yet even with his hands clamped tight over his ears, the voices didn't so much as muffle. The voices coming from The Dark were not before him but inside his mind.

He wanted to scream. He wanted to beg them to stop and leave him alone but could not form the words. Crumbling to his knees, Eldric dropped his arms, his hands dangling limply by his side.

As suddenly as they had begun, the voices stopped. The silence was nearly just as deafening. Only Eldric's ragged breathing could be heard above the pounding of his heart. As his breathing slowed, the blood no longer rushing in his ears, a great sense of wrongness coagulated around him.

He was alone. Whatever presence that was The Dark... was gone. For the first time since his solitude as the Keeper began, Eldric felt truly alone. As fear, the likes he had never known, rushed through him, it dawned on him that never before had he been afraid, even when facing The Dark in the beginning.

Before he could process the implications of his actions, Eldric rushed headlong into The Dark. Unseen behind him, the Flame flickered.

Impenetrable shadows enveloped Eldric as though he was plunged into the icy depths of a lake. Though he ran blindly, he encountered no walls or obstacles. The ground beneath his feet was smooth, clear of any debris that might trip him. With no thought to what he was doing or where he was going, Eldric ran.

After a time, his legs couldn't carry him any further. Chest heaving, he fell to the floor. If the impact caused any harm to his hands or knees, he was past the ability to perceive it.

"Come back." He choked out the words, each syllable feeling like sandpaper against his tongue.

We never left.

Gasping, Eldric lifted his gaze, searching for the source of the voice. He saw only the empty abyss. Other than his own body, he could see nothing.

"Who are you?"

You know who we are. You have always known.

Before he could utter another word, a flicker caught Eldric's attention. Turning, he saw the Flame, or what of it remained. The brazier sat only a few paces behind him, and the fire burned low, hardly licking up the side of the last log he had placed within. The light from the Flame was dim, hardly illuminating the space around him. He had run until his legs could carry him no longer, yet it seemed he had hardly gone more than a few feet. Besides the brazier, only one item could be seen in the dim light. On shaking legs, Eldric stumbled over to the basket filled with carved wooden figurines. Though he never knew who the wooden faces depicted, they felt familiar to him.

We have always been here.

As he had countless times before, Eldric gazed into The Dark. For the first time, something gazed back.

Countless shrouded figures peered back at him from the abyss. Though the details of each face were unintelligible, they were familiar. For decades, he had spent every waking moment with them. Every time he stared into the emptiness surrounding him, they stared back, calling to him.

Questions raced through Eldric's mind as he tried to process what he saw. Why had he never heard or seen them until now? Why were they there? Why had they tormented him for so long? Why was he here?

"Why?" The single word was all he could find the strength to utter, yet that one word held the weight of decades filled with suffering in solitude.

For a long moment, there was only silence. Eldric couldn't find the strength to utter the word again.

As there are those who walk in The Light, so there are those who walk in The Dark.

Hundreds of voices spoke as one, reverberating within Eldric. He could hear the voices of men, women, and children.

As has been done since the creation of Light and Dark, the Keeper must maintain the divide. One cannot exist without the other, nor can they exist in tandem. The Flame is the gate, and you the gate's Keeper. Though all must come to an end, there can be no end to the divide. Should Light and Dark unite as once they were, creation too would return to the abyss whence it came.

Silence rang throughout the abyss as the voices quieted. Their words hung heavy in the air with a sense of finality. Eldric waited for them to continue, but they stayed silent as if waiting for his reply.

Flickering drew his gaze back to the brazier. The Flame was

almost entirely gone, only the faintest blue of the fire remained, as though desperately hanging on to life while waiting to see what Eldric would do. Though he knew a decision needed to be made, he didn't know what.

Gazing into the abyss once again, Eldric looked past the shrouded figures to the darkness beyond. Deeper than the darkest shadows, he could almost see shapes form and dissolve. Goliath figures dissolved into hundreds of smaller outlines. Humanoid shifted to beast, then into nothing, only to form elsewhere into something unrecognizable.

The Dark.

All at once, Eldric understood. The Flame was dying, the gate between The Light and Dark growing weak. Two sides now stood dangerously close to combining. As a Keeper, it was Eldric's duty to keep the Flame alive. Determination, frustration, and desperation battled for control as his mind searched for the answer. He knew the logs he supplied the flame for decades were no longer enough.

A sudden stab of pain pulled his gaze down to his hand, where he found he was grasping tightly at something. Leaning closer to the dying Flame, he opened his palm. The unfinished figurine he had been working on last lay in his hand. From a cut in his thumb, a thin smear of his blood marred the surface of the figure's unfinished face.

The figurine was of himself. He had thought the talisman was unfinished, for the features were undefined, almost as if the creator wasn't entirely sure what the person they were supposed to replicate looked like, just as he had long ago forgotten the features of his own face.

Understanding, resignation, and finally, acceptance rolled through Eldric. He knew what he needed to do. Clenching the small wooden figure again, he held his hand over the last flickering flames.

The Rebirth.

As Eldric opened his palm, flames leaped to meet the figure as the Keeper gave himself to The Flame.

Ever Northward

An endless expanse of white lay before me, the frozen horizon barely discernible from the monochromatic canvas that is the sky. No signs of life dot the landscape, no distant mirage of foliage. Only an endless slab of white marred by gusting winds carrying even more snow to coat the world around me.

The sting of frostbite nips at my fingertips and toes, occasionally breaking me from the trance I'm lured into by my endless march. I don't know how long I have been traveling. It could have been days, weeks, or even a month. Time has no meaning in a place such as this. Only the pull keeps me from turning around and returning home. Something guides me, tugging at an unseen tether that leads me deeper into the Northern Waste.

Since my earliest memories, I have felt the pull. Northward. Ever northward. Though constant, the pull was easy to ignore when I was young. By the time I reached my third decade, the impulse became less of a suggestion playing at the back of my mind and more of a demand to be followed.

Knowing I could not rest until this demand was met, I began my trek northward. Ever northward.

I only notice something is wrong when I can no longer feel

the rhythm of my steps. My arms are spread out next to me, and my back is beginning to burn from the cold. I sit up, realizing I am sprawled in the snow.

Did I trip? Has my body finally given up on this ceaseless journey? Using the ice-slicked wall before me for support, I manage to pull myself up. Other than a tremble I see more than feel, my legs support me.

Wait... a wall?

Backpedaling, I find that I am facing a large wooden wall. Puzzled by the structure's sudden appearance, I slowly back up and take in my surroundings. Wooden buildings surround me. Though seemingly abandoned, they do not show signs of decay.

Where did this settlement come from? Ever since the never-ending snowstorm claimed this corner of the region twenty-five years ago, the land, now called the Northern Wastes, has become inhospitable. Adventurers from all corners of the world have attempted to brave the frozen expanse, determined to find what evil lay within. The few who returned succumbed to hypothermia not long after. Perhaps some did manage to make it through and decided to settle here, though I could only speculate on where they found the resources to build a settlement this far into the Waste.

I notice the wind has receded from the settlement as though I've entered a small bubble of protection from the elements. Though I can see the storm raging in the distance, the air within is still. Quiet. Unnaturally so, as though time itself has frozen over.

The pull is weaker now, though I can still feel the invisible tether leading me further north. As before, I allow myself to be led as I move deeper into the frozen village. A thin layer of snow and ice gives the world around me the impression that it is made of polished marble. Cobblestone paths lead me between buildings, and the farther I walk, the less I feel the pull's influence.

Echoing laughter pulls my attention toward a small bridge to my right. I pause, straining to hear. Eerie silence greets me. I cannot blame the sound as a trick of the wind. There is no wind.

Cautious, I walk toward the small bridge just wide enough for a horse-drawn wagon to pass comfortably.

~*~

A group of small children giggle and shove at each other as they dart over the bridge and around the wagon. The old man steering the wagon shouts at the children, waving his fist as the horse startles and jostles its reigns. The children either do not notice or don't care as they laugh and sprint down the gentle slope toward the stream that cuts through the center of town.

They splash into the shallow water, searching just below the surface for treasures. Another young girl watches from the shadow of an oak tree as the children splash and play. She gathers her courage, steps away from the oak, and inches toward the group. One of the girls notices her and gasps, pointing at the newcomer. The others quickly follow suit before scrambling away from her, retreating over the far bank. The newcomer, now alone, hangs her head in defeat and walks away.

~*~

A shock across my temples has me screwing my eyes shut in

pain. When I open them again, the scene before me is as before. White as marble and frozen. There are no laughing children or a wagon rumbling across the bridge. Forcefully blinking does nothing to bring back the vision I just witnessed.

I focus my attention on the large oak tree, where the little girl had hidden, and watched the others play. An odd feeling washes over me, and I'm sure the hair on the back of my neck would be standing on end had I not been so numb from the cold. It isn't until I stand directly beneath the reaching branches that I discover the source of oddity.

The oak has not lost its leaves to the winter. Rather than wither and fall, the leaves are perfectly preserved, still hanging to their branches. The slightest hue of green can be seen beneath the fine coating of snow and ice. Unsure how to process this discovery, I again follow the tether.

Crossing the bridge, I find myself in what could be the town center. A decent-sized well sits as the focal point of a circular clearing paved in stone. Along the edges of the clearing are stalls, shops, and communal buildings. Though a common sight in most settlements, it is what I spy through the open doors of a forge that has me rooted to the spot.

~*~

The intense resonance of hammer striking metal has the girl cowering just inside the forge's double doors. Sweat trickles down the large man's back as heat wafts from the burning coals of the forge. Sparks fly with every impact of his mighty hammer. Transfixed by the miniature bursts of flame, the girl says nothing and continues to cower.

"What do you want?"

160

The man's tone is as frightening as his appearance. Trembling, she shuffles forward and holds a piece of parchment toward him. None too gently, he snatches the note from her. After reading the few words scribbled there, he scoffs.

"Sending a child to run his errands. What a coward."

The giant steps away, disappearing into a back room the girl hadn't noticed before. He returns a few moments later, tossing a small leather bag toward her. It lands heavily at her feet, the contents clinking loudly. Without another word, the man returns to work as the girl grabs the bag and darts back into the small crowd.

~*~

Pain more intense than the last has me crouching, cradling my head between my hands. Once the ringing eases, I'm able to stand once more and peer into the open doors of the forge. The man is still there. Standing before the massive anvil, his hammer is raised, poised to fall. However, the hammer doesn't strike. There is no heat wafting from burning coals. No sparks fly from the hammer impacting heated steel.

The man matches his surroundings, still as a marble statue as if frozen mid-swing. Determined to get as far from this uncanny scene as possible, I turn and nearly collide with another figure. I backpedal, arms flailing as I land firmly on the frozen ground. The marble woman is short, heavy-set, and carrying a large woven basket filled with solid loaves of bread.

I scramble to my feet and try to escape from the town center. Scattered throughout the grounds, which I had thought empty before, stand more figures frozen mid-activity. As I make my way through the crowd, I also notice animals. A small boy looks to be running after the scruffy figure of a dog, who, in turn, is chasing a panicked chicken.

A part of me wants to stop and admire the detail afforded these statues, but fear and the ever-growing dread in my stomach urge me on.

Reaching the outskirts of the small town, I brace myself on an icy fence as I catch my breath. Just past the line of the furthest houses, still within the odd bubble of frozen time, sits another house. Unlike the others, this one is dilapidated. Vines cover more than half of the house, the shutters broken and hanging at odd angles. Even the cobblestone path ends at my feet, replaced by a trail in the dirt worn smooth from travel.

As my sights settle on the crumbling house, the tether's strength increases tenfold. Instead of urging me ever northward as before, I feel myself being pulled toward the ruins. I have no recollection of leaving the settlement, stepping off the stone path, and following the trail to the front door.

~*~

Pushing the door open, the young girl peeks inside. A man sits across the small space at a desk pushed against the far wall. With a beaming smile, she pushes the door open the rest of the way and runs into open arms. The thin man envelopes the giggling child in a warm embrace, blowing raspberries into her cheek as she squeals and tries to escape. Setting the girl back on her feet, he lovingly pushes her unruly hair back from her face.

"How was your adventure? Did you find the treasure?"

Beaming with pride, the girl holds up the small pouch she'd retrieved from the smithy, its contents jingling.

"That's my girl!" He takes the bag from her outstretched hands

before turning her around and giving a small swat to her behind. "Now go play. I still have some work to do."

Needing not to be told twice, she excitedly runs to a large wooden box housing toys made from wood, cloth, and other spare materials. Lovingly, she picks up a well-loved doll.

~*~

As the vision clears, I notice I'm holding a small doll made from cloth and tied bits of string. Different colored threads attempt to indicate two eyes and a smiling mouth. The image of the doll blurs with sudden tears.

Could this be...?

Turning, I search for the figure I know will be there, still hunched over his desk. The surface is covered in scrolls, herbs, metal rings, and various other oddities. Unlike the other figures I had come across, this one is not likened to marble.

Long, unkempt hair pours down the man's back, peppered with the same gray that covers most of the thick beard hanging to his chest. As our gazes connect, the tether disappears. Heavy silence settles upon us. He stands slowly as if I am an animal he does not want to startle and cause to run away. He blinks a few times, reminding me of my reaction earlier upon seeing the vision of the children on the bridge.

"You've returned."

His voice is hardly more than a rasp. I feel the cold sting of fresh tears running down my cheeks. More visions rush in. No, not visions. Memories.

~*~

"Remember, you must be careful, Cataria. Make sure you hide the coins like I taught you. Stay within the limits of town, and if anyone says anything mean, walk away. If you don't feel safe, come straight home." The thin man drapes a heavy wool cloak around his daughters' shoulders.

"But Papa, I don't understand why they are so mean to you. Don't you help them all the time?"

He smiles down at his daughter. She was so curious and kind, yet the townspeople treated her like an outcast solely because she was his daughter. Had he strength to spare, he would run these errands himself. However, he needed all the energy he could spare for his work, which was hardly enough to keep them fed and warm at night. He watches Cataria turn to his worktable, plucking a small metal ring from one of many piles.

"Why do you give them these if they are so mean, papa? I thought you said these made them happy."

He has to bite the inside of his cheek to avoid laughing at how she frowns at the bit of metal, as though the fault lies with the trinket. Plucking the ring from her hand, he returns it to its place.

"It doesn't work quite like that, honey. People come to me because they have a problem they cannot fix, and I can give them the strength they need with these." He gestures to the piles of rings.

"How, papa?"

"Well..." He drags a hand down his face, unsure how to explain the concept of imbuing trinkets with magic to a ten-year-old. "When they come to me, I hear what their problem is. Then, I can put a little bit of my energy into one of these rings. When they put the ring on, they can use my energy to help them solve the problem."

Her brows slowly furrow at his explanation. He can tell she doesn't understand, even though she crosses her arms and nods as though she does.

"That sounds like a good thing."

"It is."

"Then why are they not nice to you?"

"Well... I guess that is because they don't understand how I do it. And sometimes, people are afraid of what they don't understand."

"Well, I think that's just silly."

She places her small hands on her hips, seemingly insulted at his loud bark of laughter.

"You're right, Cat, they are just silly. Now, get going. Those treasures aren't going to find themselves."

After one more brief hug, the little girl darts out the door.

~*~

As I gaze at the old man before me, more memories flash like an onslaught. I remember late nights watching him drain his energy into the rings for people who treated him bitterly out of fear. His expression that would shift from exhaustion to love at the sight of his daughter. She was too young to see how the constant drain of magic wore on him.

As quickly as they came, the memories stopped. I remember now. My childhood was spent here, but a large gap is still missing. Frowning, I glance around the small home, looking for anything that might trigger another memory. I find none.

"They took you from me." Though he looks in my direction, his eyes are glazed over, as though he is reliving the memory.

"I began to lose my strength. My magic. The talismans I made were no longer strong enough to provide the aid they wanted. They came to our home in the night, demanding that we leave. Since they no longer benefited from my magic, their reason was overruled by fear. I begged them to let us stay, as

165

I didn't know how I would travel alone with a child." Tears fill his eyes, slowly tracing wet tracks down his cheeks. "I had no idea. I didn't know they would try to use you against me. They took you the next day while you were on an errand to the butcher. They said that you ran away, but I never believed them. I thought they - " his sentence is cut off with a sob.

"I was so angry. I was furious that after all I did for them, after *everything*, they would take away the only family I had. I had already lost your mother, but to lose you too..." His teary gaze drifts toward the broken window facing the frozen town. "I'm not even sure how I did it. I just wanted everything to stop. And it did. I just wanted it to stop until..." His gaze, focused this time, returns to meet mine. "Until my Cataria came home."

Having crept closer throughout his story, I take the final step and embrace my father. Our sobs fill the still silence around us.

"It's okay, papa. I don't remember what happened or how I came to be apart from you. But it's okay. I had a good life. I was taken in by an older couple who had lost their children. They showered me with love. I filled a hole in their hearts, and they a hole in mine."

With a gasp, my father pushes me back, holding firmly to my shoulders as though he fears I will disappear again.

"But you came back! What of your new home?"

I shrug, a tear-soaked laugh escaping me. "My home will still be there when I get back. My whole life, I felt something was missing, that there was something I needed to do. Or maybe... someone I needed to see."

Taking a deep breath to help steady myself, I step away from my father. "You need to let these people go, papa. I understand what they did was wrong, but it is time for you to leave them behind. Come home with me. Meet the rest of your family.

His eyes light up, his entire demeanor seeming to jolt with shock. "The... rest... of my family?"

I can't help but smile widely as I nod. "You have a son-in-law now. And two grandsons."

Tears anew, though this time in joy, spring from my father as he falls to his knees. Along with my father's healing heart, the world around us thaws, time resuming again.

The Midnight Sonata

Marcel's patience began to wane after thirty-six hours of being confined to an eight-by-four box. His joints ached, begging for the freedom to stretch. He hoped the delivery would come sooner than scheduled, as he was now dangerously low on his meager water and food supply. Also… he didn't know how much longer he could stand the smell of dust and chemicals emanating from the other body with which he shared the small space.

Marcel cursed as the box suddenly lurched, jostling him and causing the body to fall onto him. Gagging, he gently pushed the mummified corpse away.

"Amun-Ra, my friend," Marcel whispered. "I'm at my wit's end here, and I really need you to stay on your side of the sarcophagus." He resisted the urge to sigh lest he inhale more dust and residual embalming fumes. He had already made that mistake earlier in the trip, and it took every bit of control to stifle his coughing fit. As the minutes ticked by, he distracted himself by telling his travel companion his plan. Again.

"Have you ever heard of The Midnight Sonata, my mummified friend?" Amun-Ra did not respond. "Of course you haven't since you've been dead for quite a while. Well, as I've mentioned before, but I will kindly remind you, it is a priceless painting that was recently discovered to be the original work of *Jean-Antoine Watteau*! Can you believe that? Since the day the piece was gifted to good 'ole Jean's parents, the painting has remained a priceless heirloom, passed down from generation to generation! That is until the last living descendant finally kicked the bucket. That's when then the painting was found. Isn't that splendid? It's a little selfish, though, if you ask me. Art like that should be shared with the world, not kept in an attic where it cannot be adored. Don't you agree?"

Amun-Ra again remained silent. It was just as well. Marcel wasn't sure he'd be too happy if the dead pharaoh responded. He was fully aware that it might be a little crazy to talk to the corpse, but who could blame him after so many hours with only the mummy for company? Another bump in the road caused Amun-Ra to fall against him.

"Yes, yes, I'll continue with my story. Patience, my friend." He gingerly pushed the mummy away from himself. "Patience and personal space, please. Anyway, since the last descendant passed, the painting was authenticated and put up for auction. Who else could afford such a treasure besides Paris's museum, The Louvre, home to some of the world's most priceless artwork and exhibits? Very few, I'm sure. By the way, that's where we are headed in case no one informed you."

Little did anyone realize that the work of art was soon to be rehomed. After a brief stay in his own personal collection, he would sell it to the highest bidder. The starting bid would be higher than even The Louvre had paid. And after such a feat, his name was sure to go down in history as one of the best art thieves of his time. Perhaps fame and fortune shouldn't be his sole motivation to risk life in prison, but it was enough for Marcel.

"Oh, just think of the money people will pay to get their hands on such a piece! I'll be wealthier than I've ever imagined! I've already got a list of potential buyers lined up." He sighed in wonder as he daydreamed about how he would spend his impending wealth.

Although this wasn't Marcel's first heist, this would be his most challenging. With the recent developments in security, with which The Louvre had spared no expense, Marcel was forced to get creative, an endeavor that took over six months to plan and put into motion. What better way to gain access to the museum than to be hand-delivered? That brought him to his current situation, sharing a tight space with Amun-Ra, a five-thousand-year-old pharaoh. He knew every inch of The Louvre, having spent countless hours wandering the exhibits. All he had to do now was wait for the shipment containing artifacts for the upcoming Ancient Egypt exhibit to be delivered.

Marcel was startled awake, horrified to find that Amun-Ra had lent a shoulder for him to rest on. Though the mere thought of touching the ancient being made his skin crawl, he kept that opinion to himself lest he offend the mummy. Indeed, that would cause some repercussions in his own afterlife. After stretching as much as he could in the cramped space, he pushed his ear to the side of the sarcophagus. He no longer felt the truck's vibrations, so he assumed they had either stopped or he had slept through the delivery to the museum.

He waited in silence, listening for any clues. Hearing nothing for a long while, he risked popping open the sarcophagus lid to peek at his surroundings. As the lid creaked open, he took a deep breath. Cool air raced into his lungs, carrying a myriad of smells—old parchment, wax, cleaning supplies, rubbing alcohol, and dust.

Moonlight filtered into the large space from small windows spaced around the top floor of the warehouse he had been loaded into. It seemed his impromptu nap had lasted more than a few minutes.

Rows upon rows of massive metal shelves took up half of the warehouse space, each section clearly labeled and containing boxes, wrapped bundles, and glass cases of every kind. The remaining space of the warehouse was broken into grid-like sections blocked off with colored tape. Each square contained a different exhibit of artifacts, including Ancient Egypt, which he now stood in.

After a quick yoga session to get his aching limbs back in working order, Marcel gathered his supplies from the sarcophagus, said his farewells to Amun-Ra, and headed toward the far end of the warehouse, where he hoped to find the entrance to the museum. Perhaps it had been too much to hope that they would deliver him directly to the sectioned-off corner of the museum reserved for the new exhibit, as he had planned. But no matter, he was used to having to improvise.

While searching for the correct door, he found himself distracted more than a few times by the items lining the shelves or stacked in neat quadrants. Seeing so many priceless artifacts and antiques in one place, it was lunacy not to stop and admire. No respectable art thief could blame him for doing so, and he doubted he'd ever have such an opportunity again.

He meandered through the Renaissance era, perused through the contemporary section, and puzzled at a few pieces of impressionist paintings. As he wandered, occasionally remembering that he had a job to do, he committed many of the pieces to memory so that he might add them to the list for future heists.

At long last, Marcel found the entrance to the museum. A large sign above the double doors indicated that it was the entrance to the East Wing. The Midnight Sonata was displayed on the second floor of the West Wing, which now meant he had to navigate across the entire building and up a level without tripping any of the alarms or being spotted by the cameras.

He was ready to begin after checking his pack and taking stock of his supplies one last time. Slowly, Marcel moved to push one of the large doors open.

It didn't budge.

Marcel stepped back from the doors, puzzled. As realization dawned on him, he snapped his fingers to emphasize the apparent issue.

"Of course!" He dropped his pack on the ground and began shuffling through it. "What respectable museum wouldn't lock their doors at night? Clearly, the doors would be locked! All I need is... ah! Here they are." Triumphantly, he pulled out a small lock-pick set and got to work on the tiny keyhole. Moments later, a satisfying click indicated his success.

As he prepared to push the door open again, Marcel felt the tingling sense of adrenaline creeping through him. This was why he loved his craft. The excitement, the exploration, the hours spent planning and strategizing, and then seeing your hard work pay off. The money wasn't anything to scoff at either.

Marcel's thoughts came to a halt as the doors once again remained closed. It was evident they weren't locked anymore, as there was enough of a give that light peeked through the two-inch gap when he pushed the handle. It seemed odd that they would leave the lights on overnight, but perhaps it was another security measure.

Search as he might, he found no other locks or contraptions holding the doors shut. Frustrated, he pushed the door with more force and was rewarded by the distinct sound of jingling on the other side. He crouched so his eyes were level with the handles and peeked through the gap. As he suspected, chains connected by a padlock wrapped around the handles on the other side.

Frustrated, Marcel leaned against the doors and slid down to sit on the floor. He may be used to improvising, but nothing was more frustrating than uncovering kinks in his plans that he hadn't accounted for. A locked door was one thing; cutting through chains was another. Even if he had brought his bolt cutters, it would not have fit between the small space.

There was only one thing he could do: pick the padlock.

"You can do this, Marcey. You've faced worse situations and came out on top. Don't give up now!" Reinvigorated, Marcel retrieved his lock-pick set from his pack. It was amazing what a pep talk could do!

It took over half an hour to pick the lock, not due to lack of skill but because of the sliver of space he had to work with. And if anyone ever asked, he definitely did *not* do a small victory dance when the padlock finally clicked open and fell to the floor. Thankfully, the floor must have been covered in carpet, for the lock made a dull thunk as it hit the ground, followed shortly by the chains, which were a little louder.

Marcel paused, listening to ensure the sound of the chains hitting the ground hadn't drawn the attention of the night guard. When no one came to investigate, he slowly pushed the door open.

He came face to face with a small crowd watching him with

wide eyes. Marcel froze. He stopped moving, didn't breathe, and couldn't even formulate a single thought. He might as well have been one of the statues in an exhibit.

Several people stood across the hall from the door he had just opened. They all wore suits, tuxedos, and dresses. Most had a small glass of alcohol in one hand, and others carried a small platter of finger foods. Every single one of them stared at him with wide eyes. Some were confused and shocked. A few even looked amused.

"Are you... lost?"

Marcel jumped as one of the men in the crowd spoke. He was one of the few who watched him with barely contained amusement as if he knew exactly what had happened. They had all witnessed some fool trying to break into The Louvre.

"Uh..." Marcel snapped up, trying to come across as if he belonged there. It was painfully evident that he didn't blend in with the formally dressed patrons in his black body suit and matching ski mask bunched on his head like a beanie. He cleared his throat and glanced left and right, taking note of even more fancily-clad party-goers watching him. "Yes, why I am. I was looking for the... bathroom, and it seems I was somehow locked inside that room."

Marcel could feel his face blazing under the heat of his embarrassment as a few people in the crowd laughed. He was sure they did so at his expense.

"Is that so?" The man continued. "How terrible. I guess it is a good thing you could pick the lock and escape." A giggle escaped the woman standing beside him with her hand on his arm. "If you follow the hall there, the restrooms should be on your right."

Marcel nodded in thanks before pivoting and walking

steadily away. He wanted desperately to run, but doing so would only draw even more attention to himself, not that he didn't already have the attention of everyone within earshot. True to the man's word, the restrooms were just down the hall on the right. He bypassed them, heading directly to the lobby. He would have to start from square one on his plan to lift The Midnight Sonata.

As he reached the marble lobby and headed to the front doors, he noticed a large sign with bold letters printed across the top. It read, "Welcome, extinguished guests, to the 75th annual Art Gala."

Of all nights to have planned a heist, he couldn't have picked a worse one.

For You

"**G**et down!"
Seraphina dropped to the muddy forest floor before the last of Alistair's warning rang out through the night air. A dull thud sounded above her; the shadow-shrouded handle of a night blade embedded in the bark of the tree she had stood against only a moment before. The blade disappeared in a hiss of smoke as she shoved to her feet and lunged through the darkness in the direction of Alistair's voice.

"Over here!" As usual, he seemed to know her intentions. Somehow knowing he would be there, she extended her hand into the darkness around her. His palm brushed hers before grasping tightly and pulling her behind a large rock outcropping.

Panting, she braced her hands on her knees, willing her heart to stop racing and her mind to clear. She couldn't let the panic set in, this was her only chance. When finally able to breathe without gasping, she looked toward the man beside her. She winced at the dark gash across his chest and multiple lesions marring his face.

"Are you alright?" He gently brushed her outstretched hand aside, smiling as reassuringly as he could, considering their circumstances.

"Just a few scratches. I'll be fine."

Regardless of the surrounding danger, Seraphina couldn't help but pause and observe the man before her. So much had changed over the past several months of their travel together. Less than six months ago, he approached her villa with an offer of alliance. Having not seen another living soul in years, she had initially dismissed him as an illusion, her mind finally coming loose at the seams.

"Please, I am not here to cause any trouble." He had paused, looking around at the crumbling villa, the dead trees, and the withering foliage. "Not that I could, even if I wanted to." He poked at a low-hanging tree branch, which snapped and fell to the ground.

She couldn't help but feel intrigued by the stranger. Though scuffed and worn, his silver armor was a stark contrast to the grayscale canvas her world had become. Where did he come from? The dying world around her stretched for leagues in every direction. She knew, for she had walked every inch of what was once her home.

"Where are you from, soldier?"

He snorted at the title but offered no correction. A tired, yet determined smile crept across his features, and her curiosity grew. He spoke of a land beyond the dying forests, the rotting mountains, and rancid rivers. A land that still lived. A land not yet touched by the Shade that haunted people's lands.

"Why now?" She had asked, refusing to cling to the small sliver of hope that pulled at her chest. "After all these years, why now? I may have lived in isolation amongst the ruins of my home for longer than I care to recount, but I do not forget the names we were given by those who refused to understand."

Witches. Wraiths. Monsters. Those not touched with the art

of elemental manipulation were fearful of her kind, allowing their cowardice to breed hate and enforce segregation. It was this fear of the unknown that caused her people to struggle and perish when the Shade arrived and created the Draining, an otherworldly essence that consumed all sources of life.

Rather than contempt or disgust, as she had expected, only raw sympathy flooded Alistair's eyes at the accusation. "We have been trying to reach you since the Draining began." She startled at his soft-spoken words, glancing around him for others of his kind. His head hung in sadness. "I am all that is left."

His silver armor seemed suddenly dull, the weight of his words bringing to light the gouges and chips in the metal's surface. While she had wallowed in her isolated misery, cursing those who refused to come to her aide, this man and countless others had paved their way toward her people with their very lives.

"Alright." She cleared her throat, trying to force strength into her words. "What exactly is it you think two half-dead people can accomplish?"

His lopsided grin returned, and something loosened in her chest. Something she thought long dead. "Not just any two half-dead people. A Paladin of the Silver Order, and a Sorceress of the Dread Forests."

"Seraphina!" His whispered shout forced her back to the present. Despite his multiple wounds, concern for her was etched across his brow. "Are you alright?"

"Yes." She took a few deep breaths to focus, resisting the urge to peer around their rocky shelter. The dark, cloudy essence of the Draining around them would obscure anything further than a foot from her. Despite the pressing darkness, she could feel the weight of Alistair's gaze. The Paladin seemed unconvinced but didn't push her further.

"We need another plan. Divide and conquer didn't quite work as I'd hoped." She resisted reminding him that she'd argued vehemently against that plan from the first time he mentioned it. "Do you have your weapons?"

Patting her arms, waist, and thighs, she cursed. "No. My bow was snapped, and I must have dropped my daggers. I'll have to use my art."

"Magic."

She rolled her eyes. Despite how often she explained that her use of the elemental forces was a practice of art and not some mystic power, he refused to call it anything but magic. At this point, she figured his automatic correction was more a force of habit, rather than any real intention to have her change what she called her abilities. She wasn't entirely sure he realized he did it anymore.

Reaching down, Alistair pulled a thin knife the length of his forearm from a hidden sheath strapped to his thigh. He flipped the blade and handed it to her, hilt first. "For you."

How many times had she heard those words come from him? The first was during one of his many attempts to "make peace" with her irritable demeanor. He had found a small grey mushroom, shaped oddly and nearly resembling a flower. "For you." He had bowed deeply with the gesture, one arm crossing his chest and the other brandishing the mushroom flower. She couldn't tell if he was being sincere or making fun of her, as she had just revealed that she had been the heir to Dread Forests before the Draining consumed what subjects she might have one day ruled.

She had turned away from his gesture, calling over her

shoulder as she stalked away, "You might want to put that back where you found it. The spores are toxic."

He had yelped in alarm, tossing the misshapen mushroom into the gloomy forest around them. Seraphina had to bite her cheek to keep from smiling. The mushroom was harmless.

Despite her refusal to accept his first gift, he continued to offer her whatever he could. From odd and interestingly misshapen items he found to tools resourcefully created from dead foliage.

He always accompanied the gifts with those two simple words. "For you." As if he felt the need to tell her that everything he did was for her.

"Are you sure you're alright?" Rough hands grasped her shoulders, shaking lightly and bringing her thoughts again to the present. Perhaps she had hit her head at some point and was having difficulty focusing. Alistair's brows furrowed. His face was only a few inches from hers, his eyes searching hers. "Maybe you should sit and rest for now. Take advantage of the respite. We don't know when the next attack will come."

"No." She shook her head, trying to fling the memories from her mind. "No, I'm fine. What is the plan now?"

His eyes narrowed as he scrutinized her. She could tell he didn't believe that she was truly alright, but given the situation they found themselves in, they lacked the luxury of time. He nodded, released her, and took a step back. She didn't realize how warm his hands had been until the cold night air nipped at her shoulders.

"Since my brilliant plan didn't work," He stopped to glare at her eye-roll. "I figure we should try the exact opposite. If dividing its attention didn't do anything, maybe we can overcome it with brute force."

Seraphina didn't trust her voice not to waiver, so she only nodded. In the six months they had traveled together, this was their first encounter with the Shade itself. They had traveled leagues and crossed lakes with surfaces littered with the corpses of wildlife, both that of the water and land. Beasts torn straight from nightmares stalked them day and night, an occasional battle for survival ensuing when the beasts decided they had waited long enough for their meal.

They had been forced to learn quickly how to use each other's strengths to their advantage, as well as how to cover the others' weaknesses. While Seraphina could attack a beast from a distance with her art, Alistair wielded his massive great sword to cleave any creatures that came too close. In combat, they moved as one, at times communicating with mere glances.

Seraphina had known many people in her lifetime before the Draining. But never had she felt so in tune with another person's being.

Just as they had countless times before, they now moved as one against the Shade. As Alistair dove to the ground, rolling beneath the onslaught of night blades made of shadow, Seraphina thrust her hands outward, static causing her hair to lift as bolts of energy shot from her fingertips, arching toward the figure bathed in darkness. Flames darker than the abyss coiled around the figure's shape, making it near impossible to aim her attacks anywhere vital. Just as the last of her bolts left her, Alistair leaped to his feet, drawing the Shade's attention and allowing her to dart behind a tree, more night blades impacting the forest around her.

Back and forth, the combat was never-ending as neither side could gain the upper hand. Before too long, they found themselves once again behind the cover of the rock outcropping.

Sweat and blood dripped into Seraphina's eyes, blurring her vision of the Paladin beside her. He was covered in so many cuts and gashes that she could no longer tell where one ended and another began. His legs trembled as he braced himself against the cool rock. They were running out of time. She had initially believed their skill too great for the Shade to overcome, but she now saw the creature's strategy for what it was.

It was toying with them, wearing them down.

As she watched the man before her try to catch his breath, sweat mixing with blood as it ran down what remained of his tattered armor, a new kind of agony mixed with the pain emanating from her injuries. She had long accepted her fate, watching the Draining devour everyone she had ever known. But the thought of Alistair succumbing to his injuries, or falling before the Shade… The thought caused nausea to roll in her stomach.

She couldn't lose him. She wouldn't lose him. There was one last ability to her art she hadn't yet tried. It was risky, and just as likely to end her own life as destroy the Shade, but well worth the risk if it meant he would survive.

She forced her breathing to level out and her roiling stomach to settle.

"I have an idea."

"Thank the Order. Clearly, none of my ideas are working, I guess we could give one of yours a try." She saw his humor for what it was, an attempt to cover his pain and worry. She studied his face, committing every curve, line, hair, and freckle to memory. He reached for her, wrapping his hand behind the nape of her neck and pulling her forward to rest their foreheads together. His eyes were closed, but hers were wide with surprise.

182

"I trust you." Her throat swelled with emotion, and she was unable to reply. He hadn't even asked what her plan was, yet he would follow her blindly. Before she could contemplate the guilt beginning to claw its way through her, she closed her eyes and allowed herself to enjoy the closeness of him. In the cold damp surrounding them within the Draining, she could feel the warmth of his body heat drifting toward her.

The moment was broken as Alistair took a deep breath and stepped back, dropping into one of the many combat stances she had memorized. All thought of his warmth dissipated as she focused on the task at hand.

"Just keep it distracted for as long as you can." He nodded, again asking no questions, and charged from behind their cover. Once she heard the whistling roar of his great sword cutting through the air, she stepped away from the cover and faced the Shade, deep in combat with a Paladin of the Silver Order.

Seraphina closed her eyes and raised her hands to cup before her chest. She had never seen this done, only heard tales and stories as a child, as it was only to be performed in times of great need.

She turned her focus inward, toward the core of her being, finding the essence of her true self. All sound faded, followed quickly by her other senses, until she perceived only herself. Light surrounded her, blinding yet comforting. She nearly lost herself in the serenity. After years of pain, the tranquility was a balm on her frayed soul. Distantly, she must have heard Alistair, for thoughts of him suddenly flooded her mind.

Every terrible joke and lopsided grin he threw her way. Every odd and useless gift he gave her somehow meant more to her than any gift riches could buy. Every attempt to make light of their dark circumstances.

She called the light to her, compressing it within herself until it transformed from an endless expanse into a ball of pure energy between her palms. She wasn't sure when she had opened her eyes, but she raised her gaze to fix on the ever-shifting visage of the Shade. She was dimly aware of Alistair a few paces to her right, panting and leaning heavily on his great sword, the weapon's tip wedged deep in the ground.

Though she could see no features, she knew the Shade watched her. Could it tell what she was about to do? Was it afraid? She certainly hoped so. Releasing all tethers she had to the art, she pushed the ball of pure essence from herself and directly toward the Shade. Though she had put little physical effort into the action, the ball zipped away from her, hardly more than a blinding blur as it sped toward the Shade.

The instant before the energy made contact with the form-less specter, she could have sworn she heard a high-pitched squeal.

Light exploded from the impact, blinding Seraphina and Alistair. As quickly as the light had expanded, it shrunk, seeming to absorb into the Shade's form, now a writhing black mass of flames and smoke. As the light extinguished, the visage of the Shade exploded in all directions, carrying with it another shriek.

Her body drained of all energy, Seraphina was helpless but to watch as the blast of darkness shot toward her. She was not afraid. She had known tearing the art from her very soul was likely to kill her. She just hoped Alistair had found cover.

"Seraphina!" She watched in absolute horror as Alistair dove toward her, angling his body to shield her from the blast. She wanted to scream for him to find cover but had hardly opened her mouth when the darkness impacted his back, sending him sprawling across her.

The explosion was over as quickly as it began, the sudden silence ringing in her ears. She lay there for a moment, stunned. Alistair lay unmoving on top of her, his weight pushing her deeper into the muddy ground. His rattled breath snapped her out of her stupor, and she somehow managed to roll him off of her, settling him on his back.

Blood dripped from his nose and ears, bright red against the mud that caked his face and tattered armor.

"You idiot!" She wanted to punch him. Had he not realized that she was trying to save him? "Why would you do that!?" Though anger laced her words, tears raced down her cheeks, mixing with the blood and sweat. His breathing rattled again, and she noticed the massive dent in his chest piece. Using the thin blade he had given her only moments before, she cut the armor from him. Once removed, he seemed to breathe easier. She watched his chest rise and fall until she was sure it wouldn't stop.

Her limbs felt as heavy as lead, and she dropped down beside him in the mud.

It was over. The Shade was gone. She didn't know if that was enough to heal her lands, but at least it could be given the chance. As darkness began to creep around the edges of her vision, she placed her hand on Alistair's chest. His heart beat strongly under her palm.

"For you."

She stirred slightly at his whispered words, fighting back the darkness of unconsciousness. "What?"

"For you. Always, for you."

A tear-soaked laugh bubbled up from Seraphina. Leaving

her hand on his chest, she finally allowed the comfort of sleep to take her, her heart beating in tandem with his.

Hope's Haven

"Vic, you can't seriously be considering this."

Victor didn't respond to her, already lost in his thoughts. Scenarios ran through his mind, each with its outcome and list of risks, as well as possible profits.

"He's already lost in his head. You know what that means?" The low octave of Doc's voice reverberated off of the metal table's surface, leaving ripples in the tin cups of water sitting forgotten before the crew. Doc sighed heavily before leaning back in his seat, his heavy boots clanking loudly on the table as he propped them up. "Means he's considering it."

Serina grumbled loudly as she jumped down from the counter's edge. She stalked angrily over to Victor, the large man still lost in his thoughts, his forefinger and thumb already in their customary spot under his chin. His brows were furrowed in deep thought. Serina, though small and thin in stature, made up for her lack in height with her attitude, a fact well-known by the entire crew of *Venturina*. Her steel-toe boots clomped loudly against the carbon deck of the chow-hall. Being the largest space onboard their cargo hauler, other than the cargo bay itself, the space was often used for any number of reasons other than just for meals, such as debriefings or crew meetings like this one.

Victor was rudely pulled from his thoughts as the butt of a pulse rifle jabbed into his ribs. Pushing Serina's weapon away half-heartedly, Victor shouted to the ship's AI, "Elara, run the message again."

"Yes, Captain." Heavy static replaced the smooth echoing voice of the computer. Serina threw her hands up in frustration and stalked back toward her usual seat. The counter.

A panicked man's voice occasionally broke through the heavy static blaring through the chow hall's speakers.

"Please, to anyone who might be listening! We are-" all five crew members in the room cringed as a high-pitched static cut through the audio feed. "-colony ship. We hail from ... and have been adrift for ... a warning! Please, do not ... like us. Please." The man hiccupped, perhaps holding back from breaking down in either terror or sadness. "I say again, please, do *not*-"

The feed dissolved to static once more before ending. The clear feminine voice of Elara announced the end of the SOS signal feed.

"Do not... what?" Victor longed to stand and pace as his thoughts again raced, a habit six years spent cramped in an old space cargo hauler had yet to break. Instead, he tapped his boot restlessly against the carbon floor.

"We ain't heroes, Vic." Jericho's rough voice, damaged from decades of smoking, barely reached him from three feet away. The old man hardly ever spoke. As such, on the rare occasion he did, those around him tended to listen. Including Victor. Broken again from his thoughts, though this time less unpleasantly, he took in the people in the room with him. His crew. His make-shift family.

Doc sat at the far end of the table. The enormous man leaned casually back in his chair; boots propped up on the table. He refused to tell anyone what his real name was, or where he was from. On a ship full of individuals running from their pasts, no one questioned his reason for secrecy, especially when he proved his usefulness around the med-bay and was officially dubbed "Doc".

To the giant's left was Mouse, a boy who had managed to stow away in their cargo bay six months ago. No one could figure out where he came from or what led a sixteen-year-old boy to seek safety from a backwater mining planet onboard a cargo hauler with a less-than-reputable crew, but his innocence and drive to be helpful quickly grew on every member. Victor still wasn't convinced that they wouldn't leave him at the next respectable city they docked in but they always seemed to find some excuse to keep the kid onboard.

Propped on the counter was Serina, a small woman with more attitude than should be considered healthy. Though she was quick to bite the metaphorical head off of anyone who got in her way, she was loyal and one hell of a good shot with her plasma rifle. Not to mention she was the only person on this rust-bucket that spoke fluently in all five common dialects used throughout the Republic-owned sects of space. A talent that often came in handy when dealing with their variety of clientele. If only her attitude didn't cause most of their negotiations to devolve into fights and the occasional emergency take-off.

To Victor's right and sitting the closest was Jericho. The *Venturina* initially belonged to the old man when Victor purchased it nearly seven years ago. Though the ship was old and hardly ran well enough to make the jumps needed to get from one sect to another, the asking price was nearly too good

189

to be true. When asked what the catch was, Jericho insisted he be taken along as a crew member to keep the old bucket running. Having no mechanical intuition of his own, Victor was forced to agree. He asked the old man what happened to his old crew on a few occasions and was given different outlandish answers. Each time, the answer was more eccentric than the last. At some point, he figured it was best he didn't know.

The last member of their small crew was the most secretive of them all. Belira. The woman was tall and thin, her skin as pale as a ghost. Though bewitching to look upon, it took several weeks before the crew stopped wincing when they met her gaze. Her eyes, lacking any iris or pupil, were a milky white. Despite this, she was mute, rather than blind. And she was the best navigator and pilot Victor had ever seen. Victor "bought" her three years ago from a merchant, sickened by the laws in that sect which still allowed the barbaric practice of slave trade. Despite how many times he had told her since she first stepped foot on his ship that she belonged to no being and was now free, she refused to leave the ship. He wasn't sure why she remained but found himself thankful that she did every time she managed to navigate them out of a sticky situation.

Each member of his crew had their reasons for running from the Republic. An unspoken rule existed that none were forced to share details of their past or any insight as to why they ran or what lives they had left behind. All that was expected was loyalty to each other. Just as Victor had his reasons for keeping his head low and off of the Republic's radar, he couldn't ignore this SOS beacon.

The eyes of his crew followed him as he stood and moved

to a large screen built into the wall. He brought up the view from the ship's control room at the touch of a few buttons. Looming in the darkness ahead of them, lit only by the faded glow of the *Venturina's* flood lights, drifted a massive colony ship. The sheer size of the vessel brought out gasps from most of the crew behind him. Scrolled along the ship's side in bold, white script was *Hope's Haven*.

If not for the occasional flicker of exterior lights, the ship would seem lifeless.

"We may not be heroes," He glanced at Jericho. "But we can't ignore an SOS from a colony ship." The only response he received was the dull thud of Serina knocking the back of her head against the metal wall, presumably out of frustration. Hearing no other objection from his crew, he left the chow hall and made his way to the control room, Belira a step behind him. Once there, he nodded to his pilot, indicating for her to open a line of communication with *Hope's Haven*.

"*Hope's Haven*, this is *Venturina*. We have received your SOS. Requesting permission to dock."

His request was met with static, which cut in and out repeatedly as if someone were attempting to communicate back. He repeated his request twice with the same result before telling Belira to go ahead and dock.

Thirty minutes later, he and three crew members stood before the hatch that would lead them from the safety of their cargo hauler and into the colony ship. He would have preferred to land in the ship's bay, but the large blast doors had not opened upon their approach. They were forced to dock manually to one of the small personnel hatches lining the aft end of the colony ship. Doc, Serina, and Belira stood behind him, each armed and donning emergency flight suits, which would immediately activate life support should the atmosphere inside the colony ship prove toxic or unpressurized.

"It's not too late, Vic. We can leave. We *should* leave." He knew Serina had a point, but he shook his head and pulled the hatch release. A loud hissing filled the area as the hatch opened. Since their suite's sensors didn't go off and enclose them in oxygen-producing helmets, Victor deemed the ship's atmosphere safe enough and stepped through the hatch into *Hope's Haven*.

They emerged into a long hallway lined with pressurized doors on either side. Long, slim florescent lights flickered weakly overhead. While still able to see in the flickering light, they each turned on their flashlights. Victor waited a few moments for their intrusion to be noticed, but no one came to meet them. No alarms blared. Other than the hum of electricity from the lights, nothing stirred.

The hair on Victor's arms beneath his suit began to rise as the tingling sensation of dread crept up his spine. Before his nerves could get the better of him, Victor lifted his plasma pistol and signaled his small team forward.

After nearly an hour of navigating through silent hallways filled with flickering lights, they finally emerged into a massive open space. The group let out a collective gasp as they took in the sight. Larger than any loading bay Victor had ever seen, the space exposed six levels above them and another five below. Bridges, platforms, and stairs connected the levels at seemingly random intervals. The platforms contained all manner of amenities, from small fields of grass circled by park benches and gazebos to classic playgrounds and shop stalls.

Along the walls, storefronts complete with shelves and awnings stood untouched. Though impressive, the lack of people in such a massive space was unsettling. Far above them, a massive dome covered in thousands of lights immersed the entire area in warm light. After a few seconds, the lights would dim to a dark blue, casting the expanse of bridges and platforms in darkness, before gradually shifting back to warm light.

Serina shuffled back and forth, rubbing her arms in discomfort. "This place is creepy. Where is everybody?"

Victor shrugged, his attention on Belira, who had wandered to a stall set into the wall closest to where they emerged from the hallways. She bent over the counter, grabbed a small box from a shelf, and walked back toward the group. Victor tried to identify the small box in her hand as she approached. The construct was only a foot wide, its face littered with buttons and dials. Each end of the box was covered in a mesh material.

"I don't believe it." Jericho's scratchy voice jolted through their headsets, causing each of them to startle. In the oddness surrounding them, Victor had forgotten that the rest of the crew watched their status from the safety of the control room onboard the *Venturina*.

"What is it, old man?" Victor's words, as soft-spoken as they had been, seemed to echo in the emptiness around them.

"What she's got there. 'S a radio. I haven't seen one'a dem like that since I was a kid. Even then, it was an antique." Victor studied the box a moment longer before telling Belira to return it.

As they made their way deeper into the open space, a sudden blur of movement caught Victor's attention. Yet when he turned, he found nothing except for an empty platform covered in shopping stalls.

"Vic." Doc's unsteady tone was enough to have him hurrying

to the large man's side. He stood on another platform, parallel to the one covered in stalls. As he reached Doc's side, so did the rest of the crew, staring down at the grassy platform.

It took a moment for Victor to make sense of what he looked at. Serina understood at the same moment. She cursed and stepped back, her face white with terror.

The grass-covered hill before them moved as slight waves would upon gentle water. However, it was not a breeze that caused the blades of green to move, but time. Within seconds, the blades would grow to a few inches long, before suddenly halving themselves. Only to grow again. It was as though Victor was watching the field's life cycle on repeat.

Icy dread crept across his limbs as he understood. Slowly, now knowing what to look for, Victor turned and looked out over the network of platforms and bridges. Blurs of movement, as he had noticed before, caught his attention again. This time, he was able to process what he saw.

Individuals and groups of people raced around their small crew at incredible rates. So fast, their bodies were no more than a blur. Grass grew, then was cut to maintain its length. The lights far above brightened to daylight, then instantly dimmed to night, before cycling again.

Hope's Haven was stuck in a time-loop; a cosmic phenomenon still unexplained by this era's brightest star-faring researchers. They had to get out of there before they became ensnared in the same trap. Victor turned, his order to retreat already forming, only to find himself alone on the platform. There was no sign of Doc, Serina, or Belira.

"No. No no no no…" Refusing to believe it was too late, he turned and ran back the way they had come. Terror flowed like acid through his veins as he tried to remember which turns they had taken through the maze of hallways back to *Venturina*. The blur of motion snagged at the fringes of his vision, but he refused to acknowledge what he knew surrounded him.

"Jericho, Mouse, come in!" Neither responded to his call on his headset. Not even static.

Gasping for breath, either from raw terror or exertion of running, Victor found himself before a large, pressurized door. Silently, the entry opened and closed repeatedly, as though something kept the doors from closing completely. This wasn't the hatch to his ship, but the sound of static on the other end caught his attention. As the doors slid open, Victor jumped through the entry and into the room beyond.

Judging by the wall of ancient-looking screens, blinking lights, and numerous chairs bolted to the deck, he assumed this was the ship's control room. A dim static sounded from large speakers in the consoles lining the room. A clear voice came through the speakers before Victor could consider what to do next.

"*Hope's Haven*, this is *Venturina*. We have received your SOS. Requesting permission to dock."

Sickness roiled in his stomach as he recognized his voice.

Hands shaking, Victor searched the matrix of lights and buttons before him. The controls were older than anything he had seen before, and it took longer than he'd ever admit to any other Captain to find the controls for the line that would link him to the ship hailing *Hope's Haven*.

The wrongness of the entire situation caused him to shiver as he opened the line. It didn't feel right to respond to his own request to dock.

"Abort!" Victor nearly shouted into the mic as he responded. "Do not dock, I repeat, *do not dock this ship!*"

He could feel his heart rate racing as he waited to see if his message was received. His stomach sunk as he heard himself repeat the request to dock. Remembering that his request earlier had been met with static, he refused to accept what he already knew and continued to shout into the mic.

Eventually, the requests stopped coming. A few moments later, a light on a far panel illuminated, a shrill buzzing filling the control room. Dazed, Victor stumbled over to it. The light indicated that one of the external hatches along the aft of the ship had been breached.

The Demon Within

The force of the door slamming shut caused Karina to flinch in her chair, the chains connecting her wrist and ankle cuffs clinking loudly against the metal rings holding her in place. With an audible huff, a large, cleanly shaved man in a crisp black suit sat heavily in the chair across the small metal table from her. His dark brown eyes were as hard as the rest of his features. He didn't try to hide his disdain for her as he tossed a folder between them. She had just enough time to notice her name stamped across the top before he flipped it open.

"Karina Bartell. Age twenty. Parents deceased, no other living relatives. Graduated from Mount Spring High School two years ago. Enrolled in the local community college but never attended." He looked up from the file and fixed her with a cold sneer. "Not a whole lot to look at, are you?"

Karina's brows furrowed. She wasn't sure if he was referring to her file or plain features. Either way, she didn't understand what that had to do with why she was cuffed to a table in a small, featureless room. A wide, dark mirror ran the length of the wall to her right, and she could barely make out the faint outlines of bodies on the other side of the one-way window.

"So, what?" He continued. "Didn't make any friends in

school, so you decided to go on a killing spree?" The man pulled a stack of pictures from her file and tossed them on the table, scattering the photographs across the cold surface. She immediately pulled away as far as she could from the gruesome scenes before her, squeezing her eyes shut. "Or let me guess, you're innocent? Or maybe we've got the wrong person? Look at the pictures."

Eyes squeezed shut, Karina vehemently shook her head. The man slammed a fist on the table, eliciting a small sob from her.

"Look at them!"

Her body trembled as she slowly opened her eyes. She already knew what the pictures would depict, but that didn't stop the nausea from roiling in her stomach. Dismembered figures lay scattered throughout the apartment living room, blood painting every surface a vibrant red. Unable to stand the sight any longer, she shut her eyes again. A scene redder and bloodier than the pictures filled her mind's eye as memories of the previous night resurfaced.

Chanting. Screaming. Blood. So much blood.

"Pathetic." Though laced with contempt, the man's words brought her back to the present, which she was grateful for. "Can't even look at the mess you made." Silence enveloped the room. Karina refused to speak, and the cold man refused to drop his glower. If looks could kill, she would have dropped dead the moment he stepped through the door. Such a thought made her want to laugh hysterically. How much easier everything would be if she had died like all the others. Easier for herself, maybe, but worse for the rest of the world. So, so much worse.

The man shook his head before standing and stalking out of the room, once again slamming the door behind him.

Karina studied the wall across from her rather than the pictures before her. She spent the better part of an hour mapping out every dip, crack, and crevice in the stucco walls before the door opened. This time, the door closed softly. Another man sat down across the table from her.

Like the first man, this one also wore a business suit. Though the jacket was missing, his sleeves were pushed past his elbows. Where the first man had been all hard angles and features, this one was soft. His sandy brown hair was askew as if he had just woken up or run his hands through the shaggy locks too many times. A light stubble spread across his jaw, and she could see the deep purple bags forming under his light green eyes. Despite his haggard appearance, he couldn't have been older than his mid-twenties. And he was quite handsome.

"Hello, Karina. My name is Jeremy." Some of the tension left her body at his soft tone. "I believe you already met my partner, Clint, earlier. As usual, I must apologize for his uncouth behavior. We aren't here to call anyone names or point fingers. At least not yet." He grinned at her. At any other time, she would have returned the smile. "Right now, we just want to know what happened last night. A lot of people lost their lives, all young women not much older than yourself."

I don't believe it. They are playing good cop, bad cop. I thought that only happened in movies!

Any tension Karina had lost earlier returned tenfold as the voice hissed from behind her. Jeremy noticed her stiffened posture and raised an eyebrow. She tried to force a smile, silently begging him not to notice the other body in the room. To her relief, the detective turned to the table, and the pictures spread across its metal surface.

Jeremy gathered the pictures and flipped through them as

199

casually as one might when looking through postcards. A slim, tall figure stepped out from behind Karina and lazily strolled toward the detective. Panic sheared through her chest as she stared intently at the top of Jeremy's head, pretending not to notice the gangly form.

The figure wore a closely tailored grey and black pinstripe suit. The tight-fitting material emphasized the unnaturally thin legs and the disproportionately long arms compared to the rest of its body. Each of the figure's long, multi-jointed fingers ended in a black, talon-like point. At first glance, its pale face might be seen as handsome. However, the longer she looked, the more uncanny its features appeared. Its black eyes were a little too large, its grinning mouth a little too wide. Pearly white teeth fit together in jagged lines as if each tooth had been filed to a sharp point. Like spilled grease, jet-black hair hung to its shoulders.

As the figure leisurely made its way behind the detective, it leaned over his shoulder and studied the man's face. Karina held her breath.

So this is what you find attractive? How... interesting. Should I steal his face?

No words escaped from the creature's terrifying grin, yet its hissing words echoed within her head. Her gaze snapped to the figure as its features began to warp. Its long black hair shortened and lightened, taking on the same sandy hue as Jeremy's. Deep purple bags appeared below its eyes as the pupils shifted from black to green. Though its face resembled Jeremy's, complete with the five-o'clock shadow, the eyes were still too large, its smile too wide. Goosebumps ran the length of Karina's arms, causing the fine hairs to stand on end. Her saliva thickened, and she thought she might be sick.

Seemingly satisfied with her horror, the figure's focus turned to the open file in Jeremy's hands. Two minutes of uninterrupted silence passed while the detective studied the pictures and her file. He paused on a page with a picture paper clipped to the top. His eyes widened slightly, his eyebrows slowly rising toward his hairline. The figure seemed just as interested in what the picture contained, its disturbing smile widening to an unnatural width.

"What really happened last night, Miss Bartell?" Jeremy asked without looking up from whatever had caught his and the figure's attention. When she didn't answer, the detective closed her file and fixed her with a steady gaze. He seemed utterly unaware of the creature standing over his shoulder.

"I don't think you murdered those women. But I think you know who did. Or, instead of who, I think you know *what* did…"

Her eyes widened, and it took all her willpower not to cringe as a gleeful chuckle rang out in her head. Instead, she kept her eyes latched onto his knowing gaze. Neither said anything for a long while. The figure stood suddenly, the abrupt movement catching her attention. Though she snapped her gaze back to his, Jeremy hadn't missed her reaction and started to turn around.

"No!"

The detective was startled at her sudden outburst, turning back to face her with eyebrows raised. A victorious smile spread across his face, and Karina realized her reaction may have confirmed his suspicions.

"It's here, isn't it?" It was a statement, not a question, but she shook her head. Suddenly frustrated, she bit the insides of her lips. By denying his claim, she was only proving that he was right.

"It's alright, you can tell me."

She shook her head again, her shoulders beginning to tremble. She couldn't tell him the truth. She just couldn't. Karina knew without a doubt that there was no way she was walking out of this interrogation as a free woman, but that didn't mean she wanted a straitjacket to match her handcuffs.

Without taking his eyes off her, Jeremy flipped open the file and turned it around to face her. Three pictures were spread across the open file, each showing different angles of the living room covered in gore. In the center of the room, completely untouched by the blood and viscera, a chalk-drawn circle three feet in diameter scrolled across the floor. Odd swirling runes ran along its circumference.

As she stared at the pictures, she could hear the chanting voices from that night as they devolved into screams of terror. Red clouded her vision, the screams becoming louder. Blood soaked through red haze, running down the walls like overflowing paint.

"This isn't the first time I've seen this." Jeremy's words snapped her back into the moment. There was no screaming. No blood. Just her, the detective, and the grinning demon behind him. "This isn't the first time something has been pulled into our world. But I need to know what it is so that we can find a way to get rid of it." He held her gaze, pleading and sincere. "I know you're scared. But I need to know. What is its name?"

The demon, unable to hold in its amusement any longer, barked a laugh and spun behind the detective's back, its arms raised as though presenting itself to a grand audience.

Oh yes! Tell him my name! Go ahead, I don't mind. Tell him!

Karina knew precisely what would happen if she did. She cleared her throat, and Jeremy leaned forward in rapt attention.

"I can't say it." Her voice was hardly more than a whisper. The demon scoffed and turned away simultaneously as Jeremy leaned back in his chair and released a long, drawn-out sigh.

"Then I don't know how to help you, Miss Bartell. Unless you tell me what really killed all of those women, you will end up taking the blame."

Karina sank into her chair as he spoke, her terror melting into bone-deep exhaustion. "If I say that *thing's* name, I'll lose my hold on it. I barely stopped it last night by trapping it within my body. I don't," She paused to take a shuddering breath. "I don't have the strength to trap it a second time." She didn't know whether he believed her, and she frankly didn't care. She was just so tired.

Silence followed her admission, the rhythmic tapping of Jeremy's pen against the table's surface the only sound in the room. The demon was busy trying to peer through the one-sided window at the shrouded figures beyond. Karina absently wondered what her mysterious audience thought of her confession. Did they think she was crazy? They probably figured she was just another youth with drug-induced hallucinations.

Jeremy dropped his pen and leaned forward in his chair, the groaning of the metal chair uncomfortably loud in the small space. "Are you alright with spending the rest of your life in prison? Unless you let me help you, that is exactly where you will end up."

Karina's eyes widened at his words, the question sparking an idea. The demon, sensing the direction of her thoughts, hissed at her. The chilling grin finally dropped from its face as its features distorted in anger.

With her decision made, Karina took a deep breath that did nothing to ease the tightness in her chest. She sat up as tall and straight as she could - or at least as much as her chained wrists would allow - and faced Jeremy with her head held high. Every bit of strength she portrayed was fabricated.

"You want to help?"

Jeremy smiled, putting his perfect teeth on display. "Yes, absolutely."

"Then… there is something you can do."

He picked up his pen and pulled a blank piece of paper from the back of her file. As soon as she started speaking, he put pen to paper.

"Like I said before, I can't say its name. Not to you. Not to anyone. The only thing you can do is lock me away where no one will find me."

He had only scribbled the first few words before he stopped and looked up at her sharply. His brows furrowed, and he opened his mouth, but she continued before he could respond.

"There is no getting rid of what this *thing* is." The demon hissed at her again. She openly glared at it. Despite the strength she tried to show, tears of fear, frustration, and defeat stung her eyes. "You need to lock me away from everyone. Killing me won't work, either. If I die, so does my hold on it. That," she nodded toward the pictures of her dismembered friends, "is after only a few seconds of it being released."

His eyes widened in shock, and he glanced about the room as if he would find the demon crouching in the corner.

Stop this!

The demon jumped onto the table in a blur, scattering the pictures and her file in every direction. It skittered across the surface to hiss in her face, its mouth snapping open to make room for elongating teeth. A loud clang echoed in the small room as Jeremy's chair flew backward, the man toppling to the floor.

"I have bound the demon to my soul." Her voice rose to drown out the insistent hissing and gnashing teeth. "To speak its name is to release it. To end my life is to release it. The only thing you can do to keep it away from others is lock me away where no one can know its name." Tears streamed freely down her cheeks as her voice shook.

Do you think this will solve anything? You will die someday! And I will be free then!

It lunged for her, and she flinched away, her cuffed wrists halting her retreat. Just before its claws could sink into her skin, the demon hit an invisible wall. Enraged, it flailed and tore at the barrier.

Jeremy watched her from where he had fallen, wide-eyed and face pale with terror. Even if he still could not see the demon, the table rocked and trembled with the force of the thrashing demon, announcing its presence.

"Please." Her voice broke under the weight of her sobs. "You have to lock me, lock *it*, away. Please, Jeremy!"

Scrambling, the detective jumped up from the floor and out the metal door, which slammed quickly behind him.

You'll pay for this!

The demon continued to writhe and hiss. Knowing it could not hurt her, Karina tuned out its threats. She retreated within herself, trying not to think of the countless empty years ahead that she had to look forward to.

This is your fault! You brought me into this world! You and the others! Why should I have to suffer for your ignorance?

205

"You're right," She rasped. "We did bring you here. My friends paid for that mistake with their lives. And now, I will pay with the rest of mine."

Liberty's Freedom

Striding into his quarters, Morgan paused just before passing the threshold. Elena stood across the small space, her figure illuminated by the swaying lantern hanging from the low ceiling. She leaned over the top of his small wooden desk, fists supporting her weight on either side of an old parchment sprawled across the desk's surface. Rocks of varying sizes pinned down each corner of the parchment to stop it from rolling in on itself.

Her features were obscured by her long black curls, which had slid over her shoulders and nearly brushed the surface of his desk. Though he couldn't see her face, her stiff posture told him all he needed to know about the approaching conversation. He had hoped to put this off for as long as possible but knew it would have to happen at some point.

Morgan took a deep breath and held it for the count of four before slowly releasing it. He finally passed the threshold and let the door click closed behind him. Elena didn't so much as startle.

"Good evening, Elena."

"Have you completely lost your mind?" She hissed, ignoring his greeting. He took his time crossing the small space, each step measured yet casual, as though he was approaching a predator instead of his childhood friend.

"I don't know what you mean." His voice was steady, but his eyes betrayed the tension building within him. He braced, preparing for the storm that was her fury.

"I mean, this!" Having pulled a hidden dagger from her waist, she slammed the blade down point first into the parchment. "I have known you to be many things, Morgan, but never a fool."

He pulled the dagger from the map and rolled the parchment in on itself. Though he kept his head high and his posture composed, he couldn't bring himself to look the woman in the eye.

"This is no different from any other voyage." Before he could tuck the rolled map safely inside his coat, Elena snatched the parchment from his hands. "Give that back," he growled.

She waved the rolled map to emphasize her steadily rising voice. "No! This is different. Every voyage we've done before was achievable. Realistic. Voyages that didn't involve sending everyone on this ship to their deaths!" Her eyes pleaded for him to understand. Morgan crossed his arms and faced her fully. Anger was quickly replacing his trepidation. "This," Elena continued, waving the rolled map a foot from his face. "This is not real. Even if it were, it is not worth risking the lives of everyone onboard for some myth."

Morgan snatched the map back and returned it to the desk. He smoothed the parchment flat, using rocks to keep it from rolling back in on itself. "Just think of it, Elena." He focused on the map, his eyes tracing the depiction of islands and ocean currents. "If we find the Scarlet Isles, imagine the untold riches just waiting to be claimed! Land left untouched since the fall of Captain Scarlet, Lord of the Pirates. They say he stashed hundreds of priceless treasures there for safekeeping."

"Do you hear yourself, Morgan? You sound like either a starstruck child or a madman. Where did you even find that map?"

"It doesn't matter." He knew admitting he'd swiped it off a drunkard during their last port visit would only worsen her opinion of the topic. "I am the Captain, and I say we follow this course. Now carry out the order, Lieutenant."

All expression dropped from Elena's face, a sign that no one besides Morgan recognized. She was fighting to control her anger. He could only hope that she won the internal struggle.

"Are you trying to pull rank on me?"

Though his blood chilled at the quiet tone of her voice, a drastic change from her shouting yet twice as terrifying, Morgan refused to back down. "I shouldn't have to pull rank. I am your Captain. You will follow my orders as long as you are on this ship. Otherwise, you can take your leave at the next port."

Elena took one small step forward. "Ever since we were children, I have followed your lead. When you decided to shirk your responsibilities at home and sneak out to sail in my grandfather's boat, I followed you. When you decided to run away from your responsibilities to play pirate," her voice began to rise as she took another step toward him. Morgan took an involuntary step back. "I followed you. I followed when you, *Captain*, decided to make a living from robbing and pilfering shipping lane transports. But this? Chasing after fantasy treasure that may or may not exist, surrounded by uncharted seas?"

"They are charted," Morgan argued, gesturing toward the map.

"That map isn't legitimate, and you know it! You spent over

fifteen years studying sea charts and cartography. And yet you have the nerve to tell me that piece of paper is the real deal? Real maps don't have pictures of sea monsters, Morgan! If I had known you would be foolish enough to risk the lives of your crew for some fallacy, I wouldn't have left everything behind to follow you."

"I never asked for you to come with me." Morgan spat. The moment the words left his mouth, he wanted to take them back. Surprise, hurt, and anger battled across her features before settling on defeat.

Her voice dropped to a whisper. "And you have no idea why I did, do you?"

Morgan wasn't sure what confused him more. Her question, or the soft tone he had never heard her use. Before he could formulate any response, Elena retreated. He hadn't realized until then that she had stalked him across the room, his back now flush against the wall. Predator, indeed.

"You may be a fool, but so am I." Without another word or glance, she left the cabin.

~*~

When Morgan addressed the crew of *Liberty's Fortune* the following morning, he feared they would respond similarly to Elena. Disbelieving and convinced he was a fool. The crowd of thirty sailors was initially silent, absorbing everything Morgan had claimed. They would traverse the Southern Ocean, heading directly into the center of the unknown. Such a voyage was insane on its own. One of the largest bodies of water in the known world, few dared to sail from one landmass to another, cutting directly through the center. The voyage would take nearly three months to reach the supposed location of the Scarlet Isles, assuming they were blessed with calm seas and mild weather.

If the distance wasn't problematic enough, there were numerous myths and speculations to choose from that could just as easily spell their doom. Some believed that a massive whirlpool existed at the center of the ocean where the currents came together in a swirling frenzy. Others claimed the unfathomable depths were home to monsters of legend.

If nautical phenomena or fantastical creatures didn't send them to a watery grave, they could very well perish from starvation before ever reaching the center. Storing enough rations to feed over thirty crew members for three months was a challenge of its own, not to mention the voyage back if they found no hospitable land in the unknown. If they were to attempt such a feat, they would have to choose between loading as little cargo as possible to allow for quicker travel and risk starvation or stocking up on as many supplies as possible to survive, which would significantly slow their progress.

Morgan didn't waste time outlining these particulars to his crew. Everyone knew the stories of what lay at the center, and he trusted his crew was savvy enough to consider the risks involved. Sweat ran down Morgan's back as he waited for his crew's response. While he might be able to coerce Elena into following his orders, doing so with the rest of the crew could incite a mutiny. After an uncomfortably long silence, a voice finally broke the stillness, just as Morgan was about to admit defeat.

"Not like we got anything better to do." Boats, his boatswain and third in command, shrugged as all eyes turned to him. He was a short, stocky man with arms the size of small tree trunks.

His mood was about as predictable as the ocean in a storm. Still, he could be relied upon to keep the crew's boredom-bred antics manageable, such as a mother might to unruly children known for causing trouble when left unsupervised for too long. Nothing riled the man quicker than calling him out on his maternal behaviors. However, Morgan suspected that he secretly enjoyed it, having lost his family to famine and disease. He'd been a broken man when he stumbled upon the motley crew of *Liberty's Fortune*. Lost and with no purpose left to him, he took on the role of boatswain like fish to water.

After a few seconds of consideration, the rest of the crew nodded or shrugged. The conversation then turned toward speculation of what kind of riches this hidden island chain might have stashed away.

Triumphant, Morgan searched for Elena in the crowd. He found her toward the aft end of the ship. She shook her head once their gazes connected. Panic gripped him as he feared she might voice her dissent in front of the crew. To his relief, the crowd jumped into action as she began barking orders to prepare the ship to set sail—their destination: Scarlet Isles.

~*~

Seven weeks later, Morgan stood at the starboard railing of the deck. He was surrounded by his crew, all silent as they stared across the water with a mix of awe and terror. Elena stood to his left, a scowl firmly in place as she stared down the entity blocking their path.

The previous three days saw still waters and calm skies. The crew believed at first that their journey had been blessed by whatever deities ruled the seas. However, the still waters seemed just as unnatural as the massive wall of fog blocking their way forward. The swirling mist of vapors stretched for miles in either direction. Circumventing the phenomenon was out of the question.

"What are your orders, Captain?" Liza's soft voice came from behind Elena's other side, but he didn't turn his focus away from the swirling wall. "According to the map, the Scarlet Isles lie at least three weeks past that..." Her voice faltered momentarily as she struggled to name the swirling obstacle before giving up. "And that is assuming the weather and seas continue to work in our favor. We are already several days ahead of schedule."

"We wouldn't be able to see an attack coming in there." Fredrick had pushed through the crowd to stand beside his twin sister, Liza. They were identical twins, though their personalities could not be further apart. While Liza was soft-spoken and intelligent, making an exceptional strategist and navigator, Fredrick was boisterous and often the center of attention, especially when alcohol was involved. Though he had little concept of strategies or star-navigating, he was unmatched in warfare at sea and on land. Though difficult to handle when under the influence, Morgan couldn't hope for a better Master Gunner in his crew. The gunner wrapped his arm around his shaking sister's shoulders.

"Coming under attack should be the least of our worries," Elena said, her tone sour. "The only idiots willing to be out on these waters are us." The nearest sailors glanced between Elena and Morgan curiously. Though occasional bickering was common between the two, never before had they gone so long in contempt. The past several weeks of travel caused a strain on their relationship.

Morgan longed to hear Elena's opinion, as she was often the one he turned to when indecision gnawed at him. For the first time in the eight years since they had stolen one of his father's naval vessels and headed for open water, he hesitated to ask her for help.

As the sole daughter of his family governess, Elena had practically grown up alongside Morgan. With his father's sole focus on running the Royal Navy as Fleet Admiral, household management fell to his mother, Adriana. Her family was new to the gentry, having made their fortune in trade and raising their status remarkably fast. Her betrothal to his father had been one of politics, not love. Once Morgan was born and the line of succession was secured, his father became a mysterious figure who rarely appeared in his own home.

"Captain?" Elena broke Morgan's train of thought. The familiar tightening in his chest from thinking of his mother eased as he turned his focus back to the present, only to be replaced by a less familiar sour pit in his stomach. Though he was the Captain of *Liberty's Fortune*, a fact that he prided himself on, Elena had refused to call him anything other than Morgan. Her use of his title had appeared over the past few weeks, and he had never hated the title more than he did when it came from her mouth. It sounded wrong coming from her, more like an insult than a title deserving of respect.

"Take us in, Lieutenant." The murmuring behind him raised in volume, but no one defied his order. Before long, the *Liberty's Fortune* dived nose-first into the wall of mist.

~*~

"Captain, the ship can't hold on much longer!"

Morgan massaged the bridge of his nose with his thumb and forefinger, stifling a sigh of frustration. Jackson, the ship's carpenter, stood before his desk. The broad man braced himself on the bulkhead, trying to keep his feet beneath him as the boat rocked violently and unpredictably from side to side. Since crossing the misty border, all signs of a temperate voyage had been lost. Wind battered at their sails and caused hundred-foot swells to crash upon the deck as if in the throws of a great storm. Try as the helmsman might, he could not get the ship under control and stay the course, not that anyone could navigate under these conditions, even if they could point the bow in any direction. The only blessing shown upon the crew was the lack of rain.

"What is it you expect me to do, Jackson? Have you managed to fix the tiller?" The steering mechanism had snapped within the first few hours after passing into the churning sea over a week ago. Jackson's face went red with anger. Morgan knew the question was unfair. No carpenter could fix an internal mechanism under these conditions regardless of skill level.

Morgan sighed and stood, grasping the desk for support, grateful the piece was bolted to the deck. "I understand your concern, Jackson. I really do. But until this blasted wind calms or we manage to drift out, there is nothing I nor anyone else on this ship can do. You are dismissed unless you have an idea or suggestion that is within my power."

The large man grunted and stomped out of the Captain's quarters as best he could without stumbling. Before the door swung shut, Elena stepped in and closed the door behind her. Morgan bit back a groan. He did not feel like fighting with her today; his patience was wearing thin as it was. He knew he wasn't the only one. Everyone on board was exhausted from lack of sleep, the constant repairs to keep the battered ship afloat, and the ever-present anxiety that came with drifting through the sea at the mercy of the wind.

"I don't want to hear it." He growled at her before she could utter a word. "You were right. Is that what you want me to say? You're always right. I am a fool." He snatched the rolled map from under a heavy metal weight holding it in place. He crinkled the old paper into a ball and moved to throw it across his small space. Just as his balance shifted to throw, the ship lurched. Already off balance, Morgan lost his footing and to the deck, his head impacting painfully against the bulkhead.

Elena was instantly at his side, trying to help him to stand. He pushed her away. Eight years' worth of self-doubt and loathing bubbled up as she stumbled. Backed against the wall, he curled his knees against his chest and buried his head in his arms.

"I don't know what I am doing, Elena. What is this all for?" Morgan's chest tightened violently as he battled with himself, trying to force his emotions back down. He felt like he was trying to swallow a cannonball. The last of his control slipped at the gentle touch of Elena's hand on his back. Despite how rude he had been to her, she still showed him kindness. Kindness he didn't deserve. She had done so much for him throughout their lives, and he'd never realized how much until now. Guilt and remorse chewed at his stomach.

"This is all my fault," The words came flowing out of him. "It's because of me that we are all going to die. Sailing to the Scarlet Isles was my idea. Every voyage we've gone on that almost ended in disaster were the ones I decided on. Running away, the piracy, you leaving your home to follow me... Running from my father and his expectations. It's all my fault."

"You never forced me to leave, Morgan." He felt some of the tightness in his chest loosen at the sound of his name instead of his title.

"I'm sorry, Elena. You were right. You're always right about everything." They sat in silence for a few minutes until Morgan whispered, "I should never have left."

"No one can blame you for leaving. I may not have been the target of your father's wrath, but I was always there. I saw the way he treated you. The way he treated Adriana." Her hand rubbed comforting circles on his back, and her voice drifted off in thought.

His mother's passing had been the catalyst. He hadn't realized until he was older everything she had done to shield him from his father's abuse. The man hadn't even attended his own wife's funeral. The morning following the procession, Morgan had received a summons to his father's office to discuss his move to the officer's barracks. That night, he told Elena his plan to leave. As he prepared his escape, she appeared in the foyer of his childhood home with a handful of others, including Liz and Fredrick. He had never asked her where she had found fellow defectors. He wasn't sure he wanted to know the answer. Had she always intended to leave her home? To leave… him?

"Why did you follow me?" He asked. Her hand stopped, and he felt her stiffen beside him. "I understand wanting to leave my family's estate. Especially after my mother's passing. But why me? I'm no great strategist. I hardly pass for a second-rate Captain. Silence stretched for a few uncomfortable minutes before she finally spoke.

"We've always been together. I can only think of a handful

of memories that don't have you in them."

Morgan snorted. "Just because we were friends as children doesn't mean you should have left your life behind for me." She didn't respond, her hand no longer drifting in circles, yet remaining on his back. Her hand felt like a branding iron, burning through his blouse directly onto his skin. "Whatever the reason, I'm glad you're here. I don't think I've ever told you that, but I've always been grateful for your company."

"Thank you," she whispered. Her head dropped to his shoulder, her hand sliding down his back to rest on the other side of his waist. Morgan went rigid, unused to such contact with her. She's laid her hands on him before, usually in a playful punch or shove, but never before so… affectionate. He hesitated before slowly relaxing and allowing his head to dip and rest on the top of hers. The contact was odd but comforting, something he didn't realize how badly he needed. Comfortable silence enveloped the room.

"We aren't moving," Elena eventually said, breaking Morgan from the daze he had allowed himself to slip into. He lifted his head to stare at her, confused. Her gaze was focused intently on the deck.

"That doesn't make any sense."

"No," she swatted his shoulder, then moved to stand. "We aren't moving. The ship…"

Morgan rose as he noticed the deck no longer lurched beneath his feet. They shared a concerned glance before sprinting out of his quarters and up the narrow stairwell to the deck. Sunlight blinded them, and they shielded their eyes as they moved to the front of the ship, where a crowd had amassed. Morgan's eyes slowly adjusted to the brightness, and he heard Elena gasp as she gripped his arm.

Two miles off the bow lay a smattering of islands. Most were nothing more than white sandbars, while others contained miniature mountain ranges and dense jungles. Tropical birds in nearly every color flocked between the islands. Morgan had laid eyes upon hundreds of islands and shorelines throughout his life, both in service to the Royal Navy and as Pirate Captain of his own ship. Never before had he seen land that seemed so... untamed. There were no piers where a vessel might dock and no refuse or debris lining the sandy beaches.

Morgan turned to see the wall of mist looming behind them. They had made it. At the mercy of the wind, they had found the Scarlet Isles. Someone on the deck, most likely Fredrick, broke into a cheer, and the rest of the crew immediately joined in. Elena clapped him on the back, causing him to stumble a step forward.

"It looks like this time, you were right. Congratulations, *Captain*." The way she used his title caused a shiver to run down his spine. For once, it didn't sound like an insult. He couldn't have stopped his grin from spreading if he had wanted to.

"Lieutenant!" He shouted to gain the attention of the celebrating crew. He tore his gaze from Elena to fix on the distant shores. "Prepare to go ashore."

Chiaroscuro of the Heart

ALEX

Bold strokes of vibrant color popped forth from a flat black background. The colors swirled, crossed, and cut back, all without blending. Each stroke was individual, its own being, yet part of the whole, only complete when combined with the rest. The painting was beautiful. Masterful, even.

But what does it mean? What was their motivation? Alex thought to himself as he stared at the painting. The placard under the spotlighted painting stated the piece was titled *Influx*. He stepped away from the piece, even more confused.

He had hoped that he might find the spark of inspiration he desperately needed by visiting his favorite art museum. Yet the more paintings, sculptures, and exhibits he came across, the less inspired and even more confused he felt. He wished he could just put pen or paint to canvas and create a masterpiece, but that didn't quite work. At least, not on the occasions where he tried. He had talent, and his work wasn't necessarily *bad*, but it was far from anything that lined the halls of even his small city's museum.

Stifling the sigh of frustration he felt clawing at his chest, Alex continued his perusal.

ALARA

Bold. Simple. Complex. Each piece was beautiful in its own right, but wasn't what she was looking for. Alara took pride in her career as an art critic, and had even written articles for some of the most notorious journals and magazines in the world. Having made a name for herself, she finally had the freedom to travel and find the perfect piece to critique.

There were different breeds of art critics. Some preferred to review pieces that they believed were an insult to the fine arts, while others provided their opinions of nearly every painting, sculpture, or platform they came across. Alara, however, preferred to critique the pieces she found genuinely wonderful and deserving of being brought into the light. Such a desire is what led her to this small city's local museum, where she hoped to find a hidden gem among the local artists.

As she came across a particularly large piece, she stopped. The canvas was tall and narrow, spanning from the floor to the high ceiling. Her attention was initially drawn to the mix of black and grey haze covering most of the space. As she looked closer, she could make out colors behind the dark layer, as though she was trying to peer through an inky cloud at the vibrancy it hid within its depths.

"Well, this is depressing." A quiet voice said from beside her. She jumped, so focused on the painting that she hadn't noticed the man's approach. He seemed just as started and immediately lowered his gaze, his hand rubbing at the back of his neck.

"I'm sorry, I didn't mean to say that out loud. Sorry for startling you." The man shuffled a few steps to the side to give her space.

He was tall and thin, with a messy mop of brown hair that

looked like he might have attempted to tame it, only for it to resume its wild nature. A few locks were stiff with what Alara assumed and hoped was styling gel. He wore a thin pair of glasses that sat low on his nose. The glasses themselves were unassuming, but what held her attention were his eyes. They were a deep brown, like liquid mahogany, displaying a wealth of emotion. A light smattering of freckles accentuated his high cheekbones. A cross-body canvas satchel sat heavily on his hip, undoubtedly filled with books and art supplies. He was the personification of a "struggling artist," a thought that almost made her laugh.

She realized she was caught staring when he peered at her curiously. She snapped her gaze back to the painting, feeling her cheeks warm. They stood quietly for a while longer, each lost in their thoughts as they gazed at the same piece.

"It *is* depressing, though." His voice was quiet again, and Alara wondered if he was talking to himself or her. Would it be rude to respond to a question not directed at her? But if he had asked her, wouldn't it be ruder not to respond? She felt his gaze land on her before saying, "What do you think?"

She mentally thanked him for saving her from her internal struggle. Focusing again on the piece before her, she studied it, humming quietly so that he knew she had heard him and was pondering her response.

"I don't believe 'depressing' is the term I would use."

"Oh..." He seemed disappointed or perhaps embarrassed, and Alara felt the sudden urge to apologize. The notion stumped her. She was a critic. She was used to people, especially artists, disagreeing with her opinions. Never before had she felt the need to *apologize* for them.

"Although," she added. "I can understand how you might

see depression within the black haze." His face brightened. He stood straighter and dropped his hand, which had started rubbing at the back of his neck again. *It must be a nervous habit,* she thought.

She could appreciate individuals who wore their emotions on their sleeve rather than hidden under a placating surface, as she did. It made it easier to talk to them without wondering what they were thinking.

ALEX

I must look like an idiot. Alex mentally slapped himself on the back of the head. First, he had startled the poor woman by muttering, a habit he spent ten years trying to break before giving up. Then, he attempted to initiate a conversation, knowing full well how awkward and uncomfortable he could be. When possible, he avoided interactions with people for this very reason. He felt he never knew what to say, and awkward silences made him fidget. He'd even rubbed sores into the back of his neck during incredibly stressful events he had been required to attend.

He was relieved when she mentioned that she understood how the piece might seem depressing, but he was more curious about her impression. He wasn't particularly interested in the painting and wasn't sure why he cared what her opinion was, but maybe it would lend some insight as to what he was missing.

"What," his voice cracked, and he quickly coughed to hide it. "What do you see, then?"

"Inner turmoil." Her answer was immediate and unexpected, causing him to glance at her in surprise. "The haze is a distraction, an entity that unwillingly pulls the viewer's focus from the emotions hidden within its depths. At the same time, those emotions are fighting to the surface, demanding to be acknowledged through the haze of self-doubt and turmoil..." Her voice slowly faded, leaving the last word hanging in the air between them.

Alex stared, transfixed. He hadn't been prepared for the depth of feeling she put into her words. He had only glanced briefly at her when he apologized for startling her, but now he actually looked at the woman standing next to him. She was a head and a half shorter than him, but her long black curls pulled into a high ponytail gave the impression that she was taller than she was. She wore no makeup, at least none that Alex could tell, but was beautiful with clear skin, bright green intelligent eyes, and full features proportionate to her height, something he could appreciate as an artist who usually struggled with proportions. She was almost a work of art herself, simple and unassuming yet stunning with natural beauty.

Her focus on the painting was so intense that Alex felt a pang of jealousy. He shoved the emotion far, far down before he even had the chance to dwell on what that could have possibly meant. She cleared her throat and continued, pulling his attention from his own inner turmoil.

"That is just my interpretation. I could be entirely incorrect." She looked surprised by her own words before visibly shaking the thought from her head. Alex leaned forward to look at the piece's placard.

"No," he said. "I think you hit the nail on the head. The title is *Chiaroscuro of the Heart*." He couldn't help but be impressed. He gazed at the piece with new eyes, clearly sensing the emotion in the background, fighting to break through the overpowering insecurity. He was nearly overwhelmed with the sense of understanding as though he were looking at his very own emotions. As enlightening as the experience was, it also made him uncomfortable, as though his soul lay bare. He felt exposed in a way he never had before, overcome with the urge to move away.

ALARA

When he didn't respond further, Alara glanced at the man beside her, worried her interpretation might have disappointed him again. Instead, he looked terrified! His thick brows were bunched together in a deep frown, his eyes fixed upon the painting as if it had personally offended him. She was unsure if his reaction was due to her words or something else. She glanced around them, thinking of something to say to distract the man that wouldn't upset him further.

Her first inclination was to invite him to walk with her. The request was already forming on her tongue before she swallowed it down.

What am I thinking!? I can't just invite a stranger to walk with me as if we were on a date! Her thoughts caused her to blush, something she unfortunately had no control over. *Maybe I should just walk away. That wouldn't be rude, would it? Sure, we talked, but it's not like I came here with him. I don't even know his name, so it wouldn't be weird if I walked away.*

"By the way, my name is Alex." Alara nearly flinched at his words, soft as they were. Her heart raced, terrified that she might have said that last part out loud. "You don't have to tell me yours if you don't want to." He continued, mistaking her silence for hesitation. "I wasn't trying to make you uncomfortable or anything. I just thought... you know...

manners and all…" He looked away from her, his hand rubbing the back of his neck again.

Cute. "No, I don't mind. I'm sorry. I was just lost in my head. My name is Alara." She nearly sighed with relief when his gaze returned to hers, dropping his hand to grip the satchel strap across his chest.

"Would you like to accompany me-"

"Would you be interested in joining me-"

They blurted simultaneously, then paused, sharing a look of shock and mild embarrassment. Alara couldn't help it and let a giggle escape, relieved. It seemed they both had the same idea.

"Yes, Alex, I would love to join you."

ALEX

His hands were sweating. Did she see him wipe them on his jeans? Could she tell he was nervous? Did he remember to put on deodorant this morning? He had tried to style his hair and clearly remembered that battle, but he couldn't remember if he had put on deodorant! He resisted the urge to lift his arm and check.

What is wrong with me? His hand ached to rub at the back of his neck, so he gripped the strap of his bag instead.

They walked the isles of the museum, occasionally asking for each other's opinion of various pieces. His interpretations felt childish compared to hers, but he feared letting the conversations drop lest she lose interest and choose to continue without him. As the minutes turned to hours, he slowly relaxed. Rarely did he attempt to socialize with anyone outside of what was expected or required, but Alara made their interactions easy. Comfortable, even. He could tell she was highly educated and used to a higher level of society than he was. Yet she didn't belittle his opinions, point out his nervous habits, or make recommendations on how to improve his character.

As the conversations flowed, he noticed his attention focusing more on her than the art surrounding them. Her gait was elegant and professional, so much so that he felt as if he were bumbling alongside her. While she was controlled grace, he was an unrestrained wreck. She giggled at a few things he said, and the sound made something warm in his chest. Her laugh was short and controlled, as though she was holding back from expressing the true extent of her emotions. He wondered what she would sound like if she just let whatever reservations she had slip away.

They were in such clear contrast to one another that he couldn't help wondering why she agreed to accompany him.

Maybe she thinks I'm funny. Not in a 'ha-ha' way, but in a 'look at that weirdo' way.

He immediately dismissed the thought. He may not have known her for very long, but he could tell she wasn't that kind of person.

"What is it that you do, Alex? I'm assuming something to do with art?"

He could have fallen to his knees and thanked her for pulling him from his spiraling thoughts. "You could say that. I'm actually an artist myself. I'm not very good… at least not good enough to have anything displayed here. But maybe one day…"

She nodded but didn't look surprised. "I thought as much. You look like an artist. Oh, I mean that in a good way!" He must not have masked his worried confusion as much as he'd hoped. "It's just," she struggled to find the right words. "I'm an art critic, so I meet a lot of artists. And you struck me as one."

Alex's eyebrows rose with genuine admiration. "Wow, an art critic? No wonder you're so good at interpretation. That actually makes me feel a little better." A blush worked its way across her cheeks. "Is that why you're here?"

"Yes. I love finding masterpieces in small areas like this, giving credit where it is due and most likely to be overlooked."

"That's admirable. I always thought critics were supposed to be… well, mean." He winced, realizing too late that he might have offended her.

Instead, she laughed. She actually laughed. The sound drew a few people's attention, but Alex ignored them, enraptured. He determined then and there that he needed to hear her laugh again. For the first time in the hours they had walked together, he felt he finally saw the woman behind her professional facade.

ALARA

She could feel her mask slipping, which she had spent years perfecting to hide her emotions. She learned the hard way that, as a critic, her emotions could be used to attack her credibility, whether that came from rival critics or disgruntled artists who disagreed with her critique.

As she walked alongside Alex, she didn't feel the need to wear her mask. He was perhaps the most genuine, if not goofy, man she had ever met. To both her horror and excitement, she could feel her own goofy side trying to surface. In a moment of silent contemplation, as they observed an oddly shaped statue of interlocking figures, Alara realized how much she could relate to the painting from earlier. *Chiaroscuro of the Heart.*

"So," She said as they entered a small courtyard lined with stone mosaics. "What is your platform of choice?"

"Well," Alex trailed off for a moment, his head cocked to the side as he studied an exceptionally abstract motley of stone fragments. "I haven't found my preferred platform, but I tend to revert to still-life portraits. I guess because that's what I first learned and practiced the most, so I'm most familiar with the techniques. I'd love to get into sculpting, but I don't have the knack for it."

"Perhaps you just haven't found your muse."

"Hmm…" He looked at her then, studying her as closely as he had the mosaic. His gaze felt like a physical touch. She turned and strolled toward the opposite side of the courtyard to hide her reddening face. "Maybe you're right." He said, following behind her. "That's actually why I'm here."

"To find your must?"

"To find inspiration."

She paused then, turning back to him. "What do you mean?"

He shrugged. "I love art. Everything about it. Ever since I was a kid, I only wanted to paint and draw. I was an arts and crafts pro in grade school." She rolled her eyes at his grin. "But as much as I *want* to create, I don't know why. That probably sounds crazy, but I don't know how else to explain it. It's like…" he looked down at his hands, flexing and straightening his long fingers. "I want so badly to create something. But what? And why? I don't care about making money. Perhaps I should; it would be nice not to worry about rent. But I don't want my passion to turn into a chore."

He looked up at her then, blinking as if he had forgotten she was there. His face turned a brilliant shade of pink, and he rubbed at the back of his neck.

"I'm sorry, I didn't mean to ramble. I bet that all sounds silly."

"Not at all! I can't say I completely understand how you feel,

229

but I do understand what you mean." He smiled gratefully and lowered his hand.

As the museum announced they would be closing soon, they made their way toward the exit in silence. Neither of them seemed to be in any particular hurry. Once they stood on the sidewalk outside the museum, the sun just beginning to dip below the artificial horizon of buildings, Alex suddenly reached forward and seized her hands. She jumped, startled by both his movement and the level of determination in his eyes.

"I'm sorry!" He dropped her hands as if he'd been burnt, then gently reached forward and grabbed them again. She bit back a smile. *So goofy, and without even trying.*

"Alara..." He didn't continue. She could almost see his thoughts as they warred across his features.

"Alex?"

He took a deep breath, nodded to himself, and then exclaimed, "I like you."

Alara stared, speechless. She liked him too but wasn't quite sure that was something they were supposed to admit on their first date.

Wait, this wasn't a date! At least not at first... Did this turn into a date? But we just met!

"I know we just met," Alex continued, seeming to read her thoughts again unknowingly. He was uncannily good at that. "But I'd like to see you again. But I understand if you're busy... or don't want to... I just..." The intensity that just seconds before had surprised her quickly faded into apprehension as he stumbled over himself.

"I would like that." She interrupted, determined to chase away the haze of insecurity threatening to smother his awkward, emotional, quirky self that she was quickly coming to admire.

He smiled, shoulders relaxing as he softened his grip on her hands so that his thumbs rubbed over the back of hers.

And maybe, just maybe, he could help her break through her own cloud of vulnerability.

Echoes of Madness

"Well, this is clearly haunted."

"Mikail!" Katlynn reached around her husband's back to lightly whack her son on the back of his head. "Knock that off."

"Momma," Kalli called from where she stood next to the van, her tiny arms wrapped tightly around Lucky's neck. The poor golden retriever was dying to run around and explore, yet stood dutifully still to allow the six-year-old to cling to her for support. "Is it really haunted?"

"No, honey," Robert said, walking over to open the van trunk. "Your brother was just making a joke. Isn't that right, Mikail?"

"Sure, not like this whole move hasn't been one big joke," Mikail responded. He stuffed his hands into the pockets of his oversized jeans and hunched his back, looking for all the world like a prisoner accepting his fate on death row.

Katlynn sighed and resisted the urge to lay down where she stood and take a much-needed nap. "How long are you going to continue to mope, Mikey? We've gone over this. Moving to the country is a fresh start. Think of it as a chance to make new friends!" Mikail grumbled as he kicked at a stray dandelion growing in the middle of the dirt path. "What was that?" Katlynn asked.

"I said to stop calling me Mikey. I'm sixteen now. You don't have to call me baby names."

She smiled and ruffled his messy brown hair, which was in dire need of a haircut. Pretty soon, she would have to stand on the tips of her toes to reach the top of his head. "Sixteen or sixty, you'll always be my Mikey."

"Mikey!" Kalli shouted as she finally released Lucky. Free at last, the dog bounded off to explore her new surroundings. "Let's explore!" She pulled her brother's hand from his pocket and dragged him forward. For all his grumbling, Katlynn saw him smile as he followed his little sister.

"Well, what do you think?" Robert asked as he came up beside her. He had two duffel bags draped over his shoulders and an over-packed cardboard box in his arms. "Doesn't look quite like the pictures, but it's too late now."

Katlynn hummed in agreement, taking one of the duffels from him. He kissed her forehead in thanks before trudging up the path toward their new home.

The mansion stood proudly against the backdrop of the surrounding forest, its imposing Victorian architecture looming over the landscape like a silent sentinel of a bygone era. Built in the late 1800s, its weathered facade bore the marks of time, with ivy crawling up its walls and intricate wrought-iron gates guarding the entrance. Tall, arched windows peered out from beneath gabled roofs, hinting at the grandeur that once filled its halls.

Despite the dilapidated state, the mansion had a certain beauty, a sense of faded glory that still lingered in the air. It was a place frozen in time, waiting for the right moment to reveal its true nature to those who dared to uncover its mysteries.

Goosebumps inched across Katlynn's arms as she took in

the sight. Mikail may have been on to something earlier. Just as she could easily see this ancient mansion being restored to its former beauty and repurposed into the bed and breakfast of her dreams, she could just as easily imagine the building being the focal point of some horror story.

"Honey," Robert called from the large double doors. "Can you get the doors?" He shifted the large box in his arms, looking like he would drop it at any moment. Giddy excitement nearly overwhelmed her as she grabbed the keys from the van. It was time to unpack!

~*~

"Well, this sucks."

"Mikail!" Katlynn scolded. "If I have to tell you one more time to knock it off with the melodrama…" He sighed and shuffled back out the double doors to grab another box. She took a deep breath, held it for a moment, and then released it, trying not to cough as the dusty air filled her lungs. Feeling marginally better, she resumed organizing the tower of boxes into piles that indicated which rooms they belonged in.

Glass shattering echoed from an open doorway to her left, which led to the kitchens. A second later, she heard a quiet "Oops." She shared a glance with Robert, who stood on a ladder, replacing the entryway light bulbs.

"Kalli," she called. "What are you doing in there?"

"Lucky dropped a box."

Katlynn rubbed her temples and took another deep breath. Robert chuckled, the warm sound echoing in the large chamber. Mikail shuffled through the front doors carrying a small shoebox. He unceremoniously dropped it at the exact moment that a lightbulb fell and shattered.

"Oops."

"Okay!" Katlynn shouted, clapping her hands together. The clap echoed painfully, and all three of them flinched. "Sorry. Kalli, come in here please." A moment later, she skipped through the kitchen doors, Lucky not a step behind. "How about we take a break and play a game?"

"Yay, a game!" Kalli cheered as Mikail groaned.

"What about hide-and-seek?" Robert suggested as he swept up the broken bulb. "This way, we can have fun exploring our new home."

Kalli gasped, her eyes wide with wonder. Oh, to be an innocent child.

"Kalli will just get lost," Mikail deadpanned.

"No, I won't! I have Lucky!"

"Good point, Mikey," Katlynn said. "In that case, why don't you two stay together for this first game? And since the game was Dad's idea, he can be the first seeker."

After laying down a few rules, such as not hiding for too long if you couldn't be found or avoiding any basements, Robert covered his eyes and began counting while the rest went to hide. Though Katlynn went in the opposite direction from Mikail and Kalli, he could hear her daughter's excited chatter echoing through the halls.

Inside, the mansion was a maze of forgotten grandeur and faded elegance. The entrance hall boasted a sweeping staircase, its once grand banister now worn smooth and chipped from use. Tattered tapestries adorned the walls, depicting scenes from a forgotten era, while dust-covered chandeliers hung overhead, casting eerie shadows across the marble floors.

As Katlynn explored, she felt that each room held its own

story. From the opulent ballroom, which she would repurpose into an event hall, to the dusty library lined with shelves of forgotten tomes. The mansion's history seemed to whisper to her from every corner, a haunting reminder of the secrets it must hold within its walls.

A distant bark reminded her that she was supposed to be finding a good hiding spot. She slipped into a large linen closet that was thankfully free of cobwebs or rodents. Settling into the corner, she allowed her body to relax and her thoughts to roam. She couldn't believe it was finally happening; she would make her dream of running a bed and breakfast a reality. With Robert now an established author and accomplishing his own dream, he had insisted it was time to pursue hers.

Kalli had taken news of the move with excitement, as she seemed to take all things. In complete contrast, Mikail had fought with all his might. Katlynn still didn't know why he was so against the idea. Choosing instead to stay inside and either play his instruments or play games, he wasn't leaving any friends behind. It was a battle to get the kid out the door and to school most days. His grades weren't an issue, so she figured the problem lay with the school. She feared for a time that perhaps he was being bullied, but he refused to talk about it when she brought it up. All that considered, she figured the move would be great for him.

Katlynn sighed heavily and allowed her shoulders to sag, her head resting against the wall. She was so tired. Between the move, dealing with Mikail's mood swings, Kalli's ability to cause trouble with the simplest tasks, and battling her natural tendency to control every situation, she wasn't sure how much more she could take before she snapped. She wished she could take a nap. Close her eyes for just a few minutes and then get back to unpacking, figuring out utilities, getting the kids enrolled in school, and all the other joys that come with being an adult. But for now, she could close her eyes. Just for a few minutes…

~*~

Faint scratching jolted Katlynn awake. She hadn't meant to doze off. She felt like she had slept for hours, though judging by the light leaking through the crack under the linen closet door, it couldn't have been more than a few minutes. The sound of scratching came again, accompanied by the tell-tale squeak of a mouse. Biting back a squeak of her own, Katlynn jumped up and out of the closet. After ensuring she hadn't been nibbled on, she took a deep breath and leaned against the wall, the last of her panic-induced adrenaline fading.

She first noticed that the light she had seen through the door was not from the nearby window, as she had initially thought, but from the lit sconces lining the hallway. That was odd. She hadn't remembered turning them on. Perhaps Robert had made his way past here while looking for her and turned on the lights as he went. Thankfully, besides a few broken and burnt-out bulbs, most of the lights in the mansion were in working order.

She approached the large four-paneled window at the end of the hall and tried to peer through. The darkness of night on the other side was so oppressive that all she could see was her reflection. They were far from the nearest town, so it wasn't surprising not to see street lamps or the headlights of passing cars. Yet even the moon's light didn't reach the forest around them.

Figuring she had waited long enough to be found, she turned and headed back toward the entry hall. Along the way, she saw that every light was turned on. Hallways, rooms, bathrooms, and even closets had all their doors open and lights on. She was glad that Robert was thorough in his task to check the lights, but she wasn't prepared to spend their life's savings on the first electricity bill. She flicked off each light and closed every door as she passed.

The entry hall was just as she had left it, a tower of boxes in the center with smaller organized piles spread throughout the space. There was no sign of Robert, Mikail, Kalli, or Lucky. Maybe they were still looking for her.

Just as Katlynn began to call for them, she heard Lucky barking. It echoed faintly from the second floor, but she would recognize that sound anywhere. Anxiety raced through her as she registered the tone of Lucky's bark, which she used when protecting Kalli from other dogs who approached too quickly, and she felt threatened.

Katlynn raced through the labyrinthine halls, following the barks and snarls. Unlike before, the lights on this side of the mansion were not turned on, and every door was shut. Just as she thought she was close, she heard a high-pitched yelp, followed by silence. Racing around a bend in the hallway, she paused, panting. A single door stood open a few rooms down, cold white light spilling through the doorway and into the hallway.

"Lucky?" She called, her voice trembling from uncertainty and exertion. As her panting subsided, she heard the sound of running water. Gathering her courage, she peered around the doorframe. Inside was an opulent bathroom. Every surface was made of marble, including the sink and massive tub overflowing with water. Cursing, Katlynn rushed in to turn off the faucets, ignoring the water soaking through her flats. First the electricity bill, and now the water.

Once the sink and tub faucets were off, she noticed the water wasn't draining. She could see that the drain on the tub was popped open. Taking a deep breath, which she seemed to be doing more often today than usual, she reached into the cold water, unscrewed the drain cap, and felt inside for whatever was clogging the pipe. She shivered and gagged as her fingers brushed something soft. She pinched as much as she could and pulled free a large tuft of golden brown hair. The water began to drain slowly, so she reached back in, pulled a few more clumps from the drain, and then repeated the process on the sink. She paused as she approached the toilet to flush the hairy clumps, noticing her reflection in the massive gold-rimmed mirror.

Her arms, from elbow to fingertip, were drenched in a startling red. Smears of crimson covered her shirt and jeans as if she had been splashed with paint. She blinked rapidly, but her reflection didn't change. Perplexed, she looked down at herself.

Katlynn screamed. Red covered the floor, puddled in the corners, and stained the marble tub and sink. She backpedaled, dropping the wet pile of hair, which landed with a sickening splat on the tile. A clinking sound caught her attention, and she glanced back at the pile. Partially buried within the hair was a small silver pendant shaped like a bone with a single word engraved across the surface. Lucky.

"Momma?"

Katlynn yelped and spun to face the door leading to the hallway. Kalli stood just past the threshold, her face stark with horror as she took in the blood-stained bathroom. Her knees wobbled with relief. She reached toward her, ready to lift and take her away from the gruesome scene.

"Momma, what did you do to Lucky?" The shaking in her voice nearly broke Katlynn's heart, and she stopped just inches from touching the girl, as her hands were still stained red. Kalli's feet were already stained from the puddle she stood in, and the sight made her nauseous.

"Kalli, honey, where is your daddy? Have you seen Mikail?"

"What did you do to Lucky!?" Kalli screamed, her little hands balling into fists. Tears streamed down her eyes, but she wasn't looking at Katlynn. Her eyes were fixed on something behind her. Katlynn turned, intending to grab a towel or shower curtain not stained in blood to wrap around Kalli. Instead, she stared at a mangled lump of golden brown hair stained with red.

"No…" She breathed out. Kalli broke out into sobbing hysterics before darting back into the hallway. Katlynn shouted for her to come back as she raced after her. Having lost sight of her, she followed the path of little red footprints until they eventually faded at the top of the entry hall grand staircase.

"Kalli!"

"Mom?" She whirled at the sound of Mikail's shaky voice. He stood at the bottom of the stairs. Even from where she stood, she could see him trembling.

"Mikey! Where is your sister? Why weren't you with her?"

"What have you done…" His whispered words carried in the open space. Katlynn realized then that he wasn't looking at her but at the ground. Not at the ground but at the small body lying in a heap at the base.

"K-Kalli?" Mikail crouched beside the body of his little sister, hesitantly resting a hand on her shoulder and trying to roll her over. Her legs and one arm rested at odd angles, clearly broken. As he shifted her, her head turned at an awkward angle.

Katlynn stepped back, trembling and refusing to acknowledge what was happening.

"You pushed her," Mikail said, his voice rising to a shout. "Why!?" He finally looked up at her, tears streaming down his face, pure rage painted across his features.

"No," Katlynn whispered. "No, I didn't."

"How could you!?" His accusations echoed behind her as she turned and sprinted back down the hallway. Why was this happening? *What* was happening?

She stumbled through the halls in a daze, desperately trying to understand how her life had turned so quickly. Somehow, she ended up in the massive kitchen. She didn't know how she ended up here, as she could have sworn she was on the second-floor moments before. Snapping out of her daze, she grabbed a discarded towel and turned the sink on as hot as possible.

No matter how hard she scrubbed, the blood coating her arms and clothes remained. Frustrated, she turned away from the sink, towel wadded in her hand and prepared to toss. The sound of crackling made her glance down at her foot. Shattered glass and the upper half of a wine bottle littered the floor. She bent and picked it up by the neck. Was this what Kalli had dropped earlier?

Something dark caught her attention, which was a stark contrast to the white marble and stainless steel kitchen. A shoe lay on the ground, half exposed from around the kitchen island's corner. Not just any shoe, but the large metal studded boot that was the staple of Mikail's wardrobe. Numb, Katlynn slowly approached the island.

Time stood still as she stared at the body lying face down on the kitchen floor. Red liquid puddled beneath his head, crawling across the floor to settle in the cracks between marble tiles. It was impossible to tell if the liquid matted in his hair and leaking from the garish gash across the back of her son's head was blood or from the broken bottle of wine.

"Honey?" Katlynn didn't react, not even bothering to acknowledge Robert's presence. "Sweetheart," His voice shook, and what part of her heart remained intact shattered. "Please, drop the bottle."

Ah, the broken bottle. And her son lay at her feet, the back of his head cracked and bleeding onto the kitchen floor. This all had to be some sick joke, and she was struck with the desire to laugh and scream.

"Robert," She didn't recognize her own voice. It didn't belong to her; it belonged to someone dead on the inside. As dead as her children. She wanted to tell him that it wasn't her fault, that she didn't understand what was happening. But when she finally lifted her gaze from Mikail's body to settle on her husband, the horror she found directed at her kept her mouth shut. What did it matter? There was nothing she could say that would convince him she was innocent. Not that she could blame him, as she'd react in the same way were their roles reversed.

Something in the way she looked at him must have broken the last of Robert's resolve. Hands up in surrender, he slowly backed out of the kitchen as though he feared a quick retreat would trigger her to attack. Just before he disappeared from her line of sight, she saw him pull his cell phone from his pocket, no doubt to call the police.

Katlynn couldn't bring herself to care. Whatever was happening here, she had to be the cause somehow. Maybe it was for the best that she was locked away. It wasn't as if she could return to living a normal life after this, anyway. Not that she'd want to if given the chance.

A wet sound, like raw chicken impacting a cutting board, came from the entryway, quickly followed by a loud thump. Katlynn watched the doorway, torn between her desire to make sure Robert was alright and remaining where she was, numb.

"Robert?" She called, weak at first, before clearing her voice and calling again. Step by shaky step, she left the kitchen and emerged into the entrance hall. She had felt her heart break before, but now her very soul crumbled to nothing as she took in Robert's prone form on the ground, a large axe embedded in his back. They didn't even own an axe.

Her hand relaxed, the broken bottle slipping from her grip and shattering against the tile. The sound bounced off the walls and marble floor, like an echo of madness doomed to repeat for eternity.

~*~

"Another one? You've gotta be kidding me. They need to just tear this damn thing down."

Officer Johnson hummed nonchalantly, watching Abney, his younger partner, wrap a thick chain through the gate's iron bars and secure it with a thick padlock. The mansion sat just on the other side, standing sentinel over its forested domain.

"What happened here, by the way? It's always a family of four with a dog who buys this freaky place only to abandon it without notice."

"There was a murder a few hundred years ago or so. My Poppy used to tell me and the other kids about it. Apparently, the wife went nuts and killed the entire family before offed herself."

"Damn…" Abney shivered, backing away from the ancient structure as though it would strike the moment he turned his back. "How did she do it?"

"She drowned the dog, pushed her youngest kid down the stairs, bashed in the oldest kid's head with a bottle, and stuck an axe in the husband's back. Then she hung herself." When Abney didn't respond, he looked to the younger officer, the boy's eyes wide with fear. "Ah, don't worry about it. It's just an old story someone probably made up to keep kids from trying to sneak in. Let's get back to the station. Kick-off is at six, and I want to make sure I get a good spot at the bar."

As Abney nodded and headed for the patrol car, Johnson stuck a large, red "For Sale" sign in the ground.

About the Author

J.B. Redel, a native of Rio Rancho, New Mexico, brings a diverse background to the world of literature. Having served as a paralegal for the Navy, J.B. Redel developed a keen eye for detail and a passion for storytelling that continues to shape her work today.

Currently pursuing a Bachelor's degree in Creative Writing, J.B. Redel is dedicated to honing her craft and exploring the depths of imagination. Although her journey as a writer began at a young age, it's only recently that she has embarked on the path of assembling her stories into anthologies and novels.

J.B. Redel finds inspiration in a variety of genres, but it's within the realms of fantasy, horror, and science fiction where her imagination truly thrives. She delights in crafting tales that transport readers to otherworldly realms while exploring the complexities of the human experience.

With each new story, J.B. Redel invites readers to embark on a journey of wonder, suspense, and discovery, weaving together elements of the fantastical and the macabre to create unforgettable narratives.

Milton Keynes UK
Ingram Content Group UK Ltd.
UKHW010741300424
441987UK00004B/249